W9-AYD-694

The Girl of His Dreams

Other Books by Harry Mazer

CAVE UNDER THE CITY
WHEN THE PHONE RANG
HEY, KID! DOES SHE LOVE ME?
I LOVE YOU, STUPID!
THE ISLAND KEEPER
THE LAST MISSION
THE WAR ON VILLA STREET
THE SOLID GOLD KID
THE DOLLAR MAN
SNOW BOUND
GUY LENNY

Harry Mazer

The Girl of His Dreams

Thomas Y. Crowell New York

The Girl of His Dreams

 Printed in the United States of America. For information address Thomas Y. Crowell Junior Books, 10 East 53rd Street, New York, N.Y. 10022. Published simultaneously in Canada by Fitzhenry & Whiteside Limited, Toronto.

Typography by Joyce Hopkins

1 2 3 4 5 6 7 8 9 10

First Edition

Library of Congress Cataloging-in-Publication Data

Mazer, Harry.

The girl of his dreams.

Summary: Willis is ready to fall in love, but when Sophie comes into his life, and falls in love with him he's not sure if she really is the girl of his dreams.

I. Title.

PZ7.M47397Gi 1987 [Fic] 86-47749

ISBN 0-690-04640-5

ISBN 0-690-04642-1 (lib. bdg.)

To the girl who was there
when I came out from under the car
and stayed . . .

One

He ran. The night flowed past him. No thoughts, no words, no need for words. The air flowing through him. Fluid, like water. Like music. Exactly like music. Thoughts brushed aside. Only the wind in his ears, the light drag of his breath and the steady tap of his feet.

He ran because he loved to. Always alone. Never on a team. Never with other people. Never companionably, comfortably. Never running in a group, a gang.

He ran because he had to run. Running, he felt whole, complete, at peace. He ran and dreamed of fame and of a girl.

Someday he would see her. Someday he would be discovered. He was nobody now. Someday he would be somebody. He was invisible now. Someday he would be visible. Willis Pierce, the greatest miler.

The fans on their feet, shouting, Pierce! Pierce! Pierce!

And her, the girl of his dreams, waiting for him.

Two

What Willis liked to do at night was lie on the mattress in his room and listen to Doris giving advice on the radio. Sometimes he heard the sigh of a passing bus or truck, or the voices of the other tenants coming dimly through the walls. On the radio, the callers waited patiently to talk to Doris. Male and female, young and old, sad voices and grateful voices. They filled the room around him. Even the cheerful callers had sad stories. "Hello, Doris, remember me? I'm the guy in the telephone booth in the Twin Cities."

"Oh, sure I do. You've got a great voice."

"I'm lonely. I'm shy. I don't go to bars. How do I get to meet a girl?"

And Willis—what would he say if he called Doris? The man in the phone booth could have been him, though he'd never admit he was shy for the whole world to hear. Not shy—a loner. He kept to himself; he steered clear of people. He liked it that way. He liked living alone, in his own apartment, doing things his own way, not having to answer to anyone. He liked running alone. In the shop, he even liked working alone.

He didn't think of himself as someone who didn't like people. He was just more comfortable being by himself. With other people, he was on guard. He didn't want to make a fool of himself. He'd been that way all his life.

"Are you crazy?" Doris was saying to a caller.

She got a lot of kooky calls. A man wanted to be a husband to two women. A woman said that her husband was upset because the dog got into bed with them every night.

"Keep that dog out of your bed," Doris said.

"You tell her, Doris," Willis agreed.

A man called in to ask if a move to Fort Lauderdale was a good way to meet women. Doris thought so. "If you're not happy with things where you are, go someplace else."

"What about me?" Willis said. "Should I move?"

Doris, there's a girl I can't stop thinking about. She's in my dreams.

That's wonderful. Tell me about her. What is she like? What does she look like?

She has wonderful hair. It's curly and full of light, and she has this great body and she has the sort of eyes you can look into forever and never get tired.

The girl of your dreams. That's wonderful. Remember, though, dreams are one thing. Reality is something else.

How do I meet her, Doris? Where do I go? I don't go to bars. I work and I run.

You run? How do you mean? I hope you're not running away from relationships?

I'm a runner. I train. I'm an athlete. I work out, I don't meet a lot of girls.

Don't you meet any girls running? Why don't you talk to them? If you want to meet her you will meet her.

When?

I can't answer that. That's up to you. You can't get discouraged. That wonderful girl you're dreaming about is out there.

Where, Doris? I want her so much.

Walking on the street, or downtown or running in the park, he noticed every woman, every girl coming toward him. Was that her? Was that her? Was that her?

He was awake the moment he heard the click of the alarm. Sitting up. His hand flat on the top of the clock. He sat there for a moment, listening to the sounds of the house, cooling his feet on the bare floor, letting the cold touch his naked body, his bare skin. The room was still in shadows, the only light the gray from outside.

The room was austere, stripped down, bare. Mattress on the floor, radio and clock beside it. *Runners' World* magazines stacked in a corner next to the TV, posters of Aaron Hill on the wall.

Sunday morning. "Are you going to run today?" He talked to himself. Sure I'm going to run, don't I run every morning? Then go. Okay, don't push. I'm getting there.

He massaged his toes, then stood and stretched. He never stretched without feeling that he was growing taller. In junior high he had been one of the shortest boys in the class, but he'd made up for it in high school. He wasn't tall, but he wasn't short, either. Still, as he stretched, he had that old fantasy that if he stretched hard enough he could make himself grow taller.

In the bathroom he splashed cold water on himself, then peered at himself in the mirror as he slipped on his sweats. What would *she* see? Would she like him? He examined his forehead, the distance from his eyebrows to the hairline. Was his hair thinning? Was his mouth too soft? He thinned his lips, but the moment he relaxed them, the softness returned.

He pushed his bare feet into sneakers, put on his Raleigh biking cap and walked around eating from a box of breakfast cereal. "Okay, Mom, I know. I'm not eating enough to fill a rat's hole."

Outside, he turned his cap around and zipped up his sweat jacket. The landlord's small aluminum trailer was parked in the driveway. He never saw it without thinking of his parents in the trailer park near Asheville. A year ago, the doctor had told his father that he had emphysema—that was the cigarettes—and that his liver was a mess from all the drinking he'd done. If he wanted to live, he had to stop smoking and drinking. Willis never thought his father would do it. He'd seen his father stop too many times before and then go back.

But just like that, his father stopped. One day he was smoking and drinking, and the next day it was over. It wasn't just the doctor's warning. His father, who had been a welder all his life, couldn't lift anymore, and the welding fumes made him cough uncontrollably. Plus he couldn't take the winters up north anymore. He took a disability retirement, and as soon as Willis graduated high school, they all moved down to Asheville.

His parents found work in a restaurant where his mother was a waitress and Dad was her busboy. The only work Willis could find was in fast-food joints.

The three of them lived in that little trailer. His parents

in back and him in front on a pullout bed. He hated it, lying there at night listening to his father turn and groan and cough, and cough and spit. After six weeks Willis couldn't take it anymore. He wanted to go back home and he felt like a traitor saying it. His mother had always depended on him. What if his father started drinking? What if he collapsed and she needed Willis?

"Go," his mother said. "We're all right." Mother and son never talked much, but they understood each other. "Go home," she said. "If I need you, you won't be that far away."

He went, happy to go, guilty but glad. He headed home, straight for his old neighborhood, but he couldn't find a place he could afford. He found an apartment, finally, nearer downtown on Central Avenue. One room and a kitchen in a small building down below the university. His windows overlooked the big air vents behind McDonald's. His apartment always smelled like hamburger.

Transportation was good. He could catch a bus on the corner anytime to get him over to his job. His father had told him to go to Consolidated Conveyer on Spring Street, where he was hired as general labor.

For the first time in his life he was totally on his own. There was nothing he had to do. Nobody he had to answer to. He didn't have to worry if his mother needed him. Or if his father was sober. He was free of all that. He could do what he wanted, when he wanted.

He went to midnight movies, did his laundry at three in the morning, ate out a lot. He hung out in the mall, downstairs by the ice-cream stand, watching the girls. But what he mostly did was work and run. Work so he could eat. Eat so he could run. And run so he could feel good.

Now, he ran past the closed McDonald's. A bundle of

newspapers had been thrown down by the door. The bagel shop was open. A man in baggy work clothes stood outside with a carton of coffee. The winter snow was gone, but the streets were still white with salt.

A black woman and a man dressed for church were on the corner. Nearby, a couple in identical green sweatshirts had their arms around each other. Willis's eyes were drawn to couples. He straightened up and touched his cap. Would it ever be him? Would he ever be the other half of a pair?

At the field house, he did a few laps around the track. He ran well, his body motionless except for his arms and legs rotating like the spokes of a wheel. He was heated up and loose and got into a happy fantasy, imagining himself running with Aaron Hill.

Aaron Hill had been his idol ever since high school. Even then people had come out to see him run. Willis had followed Aaron Hill's career at Villanova and then at the Olympic trials, and at every AAU meet. The sports-writers said Hill hadn't achieved his potential yet, hadn't peaked. They compared him to Jim Ryun. There were all kinds of stories about Hill. They said he was part Indian and that he trained barefoot.

Willis swung in behind another runner. The college boy kicked a little, and they were off, going hot after each other. They could have been part of the same squad: They wore the same sneakers, the same mismatched sweats. After a few laps, the college boy dropped out.

Willis passed a girl with a chestnut ponytail. The pony-tail swung from shoulder to shoulder. He liked the way she ran—not pushing, not hard, just moving easily along. He sneaked a look at her and then he kicked a little, showed off, showed her his stuff. Talk, Doris had said. Next time around. Maybe.

He came up behind her again. What should he say? It should be something easy and natural. They were both runners. They had something in common. *Been running long?* Would that impress her? Maybe he should just get in stride with her and smile, no words, no awkward talk, just the two of them running together.

Then he was beside her. "Hi," he said, but he said it under his breath and so softly he wasn't sure he'd said it at all. And then he was past her, not daring to look back. What if she had talked to him? What would he have said? What would he have done?

What would Doris have said? You're not running away, are you? No, he was just running. Ponytail wouldn't have talked to him, anyway.

He left the track, ran past the double row of college fraternity houses, then down the crowded streets, past the dorms and down the hill and across Central Avenue and over to where he used to live on Villa Street.

This was his city. He knew where the ballpark was and where you could get the best hot dog and the freshest bread. It was good to go down the familiar streets, to pass his old school and think of the kids he used to know and wonder where they'd gone. The neighborhood hadn't changed that much. The same buildings, the same stores, the same billboards on the roofs. And everywhere he looked, he saw *her*, the girl of his dreams, smiling down at him from the billboards and the walls, smiling at him from posters and from twenty different magazines plastered around the newsstand.

She was soft, her eyes round and highlighted with good makeup, her lips full and moist and slightly parted, her hair framing her face. Someday he was going to see her.

He'd be turning a corner or coming out of a building and she would be there.

He would see her and she would see him. He would know and she would know. The longing would be in his eyes and in her eyes. They wouldn't speak. Maybe they would smile a little. There would be a stillness between them. They would speak to one another through their stillness. Her eyes on him and his eyes on her. Only their eyes speaking, dark and full of longing and recognition.

Three

On a dirt road, a fawn-colored dog, a boxer, was following a sturdy, wide-shouldered girl carrying a heavy suitcase. Her hair whipped across her face. A round face, eyes half closed against the wind, cheeks burning. Red cheeks, her brother often said, like a tomato. An insult? Or a farmer's compliment?

This morning, her brother had said, "Wait up, Sophie. I'll drive you. It's just going to take a minute to throw on a load of posts." His eyes were narrow and guilty, the same look he'd had when he was a kid and had done something mean to her. "Now don't move, Soph," he said. "A minute, okay?"

But of course she had moved. When had she waited for Floyd?

She shifted the suitcase from one hand to the other. It was an old-fashioned, square yellow case that she'd taken down from the attic. It was heavy now with the little china animals she collected. She was leaving, taking everything she valued with her. She wore her good jeans and a pretty blouse. She would have been smart to wear a warm sweater but she hadn't wanted to hide her blouse. Floyd had offered her his nylon school jacket. "Keep it," he said, but she refused. She didn't want anything from him or Pat, either.

When she told them she was leaving, they acted so surprised. Why? There was plenty of room for all of them here. Had they done anything? Oh, stay, they said.

But she knew. She was sensitive to the way people really felt. They wanted her out. Not that they said anything, but she felt the change in them. Little things—averted glances, a silence falling between them when she entered the room.

It all came clear that day in the kitchen when Floyd, with that guilty smile, said, "Pat's pregnant again." And Pat sitting there, shelling peas, not saying a word. Letting Floyd do all the talking. "That makes number three." What was he telling Sophie for? She could count. And then he was talking about converting the upstairs room—her room—into a nursery. "We'll fix a room over the garage for you, Soph."

Sophie would always remember the sound of peas rattling into the pan. Pat had been so eager to get the upstairs room that the next day she'd emptied Sophie's room, taken everything from the bureau and the closet, taken her china animals, her drawings and watercolors off the wall and stuffed everything into a plastic bag, then let the bag fall down the stairs.

Sophie used to love her brother. He was still her brother, but she didn't know how she felt about him. For years it had been the two of them, their mother dead and their father making life so miserable for Floyd, he ran away from home when he was fourteen. The day before he ran away, she hugged him, then bit his ear. "Don't forget me."

"What're you talking about?" He held his ear. The next day he was gone. He went to live with a farmer on the other side of Pierrepont. When he came back home at the end of the school year, he and their father started fighting again. Floyd left again.

When her father died suddenly—it was his heart—Sophie was alone for weeks, running the farm herself. It would be a while before Floyd came home. She stopped going to school. The school bus came and went before she'd finished the morning chores.

She was milking the cows every day. She had to get the milk ready for the co-op milk truck. She cleaned the cows' udders, connected the milking machine to their teats, grained the cows and cleaned out the stalls and mucked out the barn. Every day it was the same.

She was lonely. She was alone. Working too hard.

One day, loading the wheelbarrow, she found herself dreaming about flying. Her boots in muck, a shovel in her hand, and she was dreaming about flying. In an airplane! It was an old dream, a private dream that she had never shared with anyone. Big, solid Sophie flying? They would have laughed at her. "With you in it," she could hear her brother saying, "the plane wouldn't even get off the ground." She kept her dreams to herself. Sometimes she dreamed about flying over the house and the trees, sometimes she dreamed about flying an airplane.

Her father had left her a little money. That day, after she finished her chores, she drove the truck to the flying field just below Watertown, took the trial lesson, then signed up for the whole course.

The first day, the instructor had her take the plane off the ground and land it. She loved it. She wasn't the least bit scared. It was scarier climbing up inside the empty silo. She started dreaming about getting enough hours to get a pilot's license someday and then maybe have her own plane. She loved everything about flying, but most of all being above the ground, looking down and seeing the world laid out in squares and rectangles, the white fields and the black roads and the little buildings and the frozen ponds. She hated to come down. Landing was the one thing she did poorly.

When Floyd came home, everything changed. There was no time or money for more lessons. Not that Floyd made her stop, but there were so many things they needed on the farm. Their father had never been much of a farmer. He'd let things run down. Floyd had learned a lot over in Pierrepont; he was full of ideas that he wanted to try, to improve the farm.

Sophie went back to the airfield a few times, just to watch, but she didn't go up again and after a while she stopped going altogether.

She and Floyd ran the farm together. It was a happy time. When a cow freshened, they took turns sleeping in the barn. Floyd delivered the calves. Sophie drove the tractor. They shared everything fifty-fifty. Floyd said he could work with her better than he could with any man.

Then Pat moved in with Floyd. They all said it wasn't going to be any different. The three of them were going to be like one family. They all worked together. It was supposed to be the same even after Floyd and Pat got married, but it never was. Now, Floyd and Pat were the family. They ran the farm. They made the decisions.

Then the babies started coming, first Alice and then

Benjamin, and the house got crowded. Sophie didn't care. She loved the babies. And now another baby was coming . . . and they didn't have room for her anymore.

Jupiter walked with Sophie all the way to the crossroads, his big, hot body a comfort. He ran ahead, then came back. "Jupiter, Jupiter." His ears perked up each time she said his name. At the crossroads, at Park's Chevron station, she sat on her suitcase with Jupiter between her knees. She hugged him and kissed his cool nose.

Cathy Parks was at the station window, watching Sophie. She and Cathy had been best friends when they were little. They lived close, only a mile separated their houses, and they were the same age. In fifth grade, Cathy stopped sitting with her. One of the other girls made sure Sophie knew exactly why. "Cathy says you're from an ignorant family and you smell like a cow flop."

Floyd's car came off their road, trailing a cloud of dust. He circled the gas pumps and pulled up in front of her. Jupiter stood up, his tail banging into Sophie's leg.

"What did you run off for?" Floyd said. "I said I'd take you."

Take her? She didn't want to be taken. She was leaving. She made circles and arrows in the dirt with a stick. She wished he hadn't come. Everything that had to be said had been said at the house.

"Come on, Soph." Floyd had two ways of talking to her. One was ordering her around like she was two years old, and the other was wheedling, like he was two years old. This was wheedling time. "Come on, Soph, you're not going away mad, are you?"

She looked up and smiled, gave him all the smile she had, the smile he always said was wider than a barn door.

"How are you fixed for money, Soph?"

"I have enough." she said.

He insisted on pushing a roll of bills into her hand. "You have any trouble, anybody bothers you . . . I don't know what you're going down there for. You could stay here with us."

"Where? In the garage?"

"What's wrong with that? I said I'd fix it up."

Then she did something childish, couldn't help herself. She stuck out her tongue.

On the bus, she caught a glimpse of Floyd turning up their road. She looked at the wad of bills he'd given her. A lot of money, more cash than he could afford to part with. As soon as she could, she'd pay him back.

The bus went past Hefner's vegetable stand, closed now, and the B&B Diner, with a row of pickups parked out in front. After that, the sprawling brick Central School, and then it was just fields.

Sophie took out her sandwich, but left it unopened in her lap. She was going. She was glad to be going and sorry she was leaving. When would she be back? Would she be back? She was leaving the place she'd never left before, the only home she'd ever known.

Four

That same morning, Willis was late starting his run. He had to hustle if he was going to get to work on time. Come into work late once, and they looked at you. The second time you got a warning, and the third time it was the gate. He took a shortcut home along Butternut Creek. Just off Hamilton Parkway, he noticed what he thought was a plastic Clorox bottle near the water. But then it moved, and he thought it was a bird. A gull, maybe. There were a lot of gulls around the city. But it wasn't a bird. It was a plastic bag, and it was moving.

He scrambled down the embankment. The top of the bag was wired shut. He opened it gingerly. Inside there was a puppy with its legs wired together. The wires had cut right down to the bone. The dog's eyes were shut and it smelled awful. As he squatted there, a little sick and unsure of what to do, the puppy opened a large, bloodshot eye and looked straight at him. It must have been in a lot of pain, but it didn't make a sound.

It was nasty taking the wires off the dog's legs. Willis wet a piece of newspaper in the stream and washed off the worst of the mess. Then he cupped water in his hands for the dog to drink. There was nothing else he could do for it. "Sorry, pup," he said, and the dog lifted its head and smiled at him. The damned dog was dying and smiling.

What was he supposed to do now? He looked around for something to cover it with. He wasn't the SPCA. If he took the dog home, it would die on him. What was he going to do with a dead dog? But he had to do something. He couldn't just sit here looking at it. He had to get to work. So he wrapped the dog in newspaper and took it home.

In the apartment, he put the dog in the bathtub on an old rug. "I've got to go to work. If I don't see you again, I'm sorry." He left a pan of water next to it.

On Spring Street, near the plant, he stopped to buy a sub at the diner, then grabbed a paper at the newsstand and dashed down the stairs to the underground tunnel that led to the plant. He got there just as the warning whistle blew. He punched in two minutes late. Late enough for a dirty look, but not late enough for a reprimand.

Five

Sophie stood outside the bus station. The street was an ant heap of smoking, honking, snorting cars and buses. She edged past a line of yellow cabs. "Cab, miss?" A fat man grabbed her suitcase. She pulled it free. Another cabbie had the door open and reached for her arm. "Going up to the college? Cab, miss? Miss! Miss!"

Sophie kept moving. She was going to sock the next guy who tried to grab her. When the light changed, she crossed the street. People, more people, so many people on the street, rushing in and out of buildings. Everyone going somewhere, everything in motion.

She was in motion, too, but where was she going? Where would she stay tonight? When she looked up, the buildings leaned and threatened and made her dizzy. She stopped. People glanced at her. Someone elbowed her aside. Her suitcase banged into a woman. "Excuse me," Sophie said, "Can you tell me where—?"

The woman darted around her. A man trying to get

around her stepped one way, then the other. "Excuse me," Sophie said. It was like a dance. Step left, step right, then he rushed past her. Nobody had any time for her.

She fell. She didn't know how it happened. One minute she was standing and the next she was down on the sidewalk. A man offered her his hand and started to haul her up. "Don't!" She felt humiliated. She didn't need any help.

She escaped down a side street. For a while she stood against a building, the suitcase behind her, catching her breath. Across the street, there was a supermarket, the week's specials posted in the windows. She crossed the street and went in. The market was bigger and more crowded than the one at home, but it looked friendly and familiar.

She maneuvered her suitcase down the aisles, picked up a package of sandwich cremes and went looking for the dairy case. A woman with a baby in a shopping cart and another child in tow nudged Sophie. "Reach me that half gallon of milk, honey."

"This one?" Sophie handed her the carton. The woman took it, then ran after her little girl, who had disappeared around the corner. The baby in the cart looked at Sophie, then squeezed its eyes shut and howled. "Come on, baby," Sophie said. She bent over so she wouldn't look so big and frightening. "Don't be afraid. Your mommy is coming right back."

A moment later, the woman returned, dragging her little girl by the hand. She popped her into the shopping cart next to the baby. "Now you stay there, Jessie." Jessie reached out and pulled down a display of paper towels.

"Look what you did!" her mother said. Paper towels spilled across the aisle. Sophie helped the mother pick them up and restack them.

"Look what you made this nice girl do, Jessie! Thank you," she said to Sophie. "That's the last time I take you shopping with me, Jessie." She pointed to Sophie's suitcase. "That's what I ought to do. Pack a suitcase and leave. You hear that, Jessie? You're driving me crazy." She turned to Sophie. "You don't have any kids yet, do you? Don't."

She wore a pink jacket and white sneakers. Her hair was parted in the middle and caught in two braids. She looked too young to have kids of her own. Jessie had braids just like her mother's.

"I like babies," Sophie said. "My sister-in-law has two, a boy and a girl. Alice and Benjamin. She's going to have another one any day now." She was relieved to have someone to talk to. She was talking too much. "They want a boy, but I'm hoping for another girl."

"Don't hope for a Jessie if you want your sister-in-law to stay sane." She straightened Jessie's collar.

"I'm new here," Sophie said. "I just got here. I'm Sophie Browne." She put her hand on the shopping cart. "Do you know where I can find a place to live?"

"Don't you know anybody?"

"I know you," Sophie said hopefully.

"A lot of good that'll do you. What'd you say your name is? Sophie Browne? Cute. My name's Brenda Leonard. Listen, Sophie, wait for me by the checkout—I'll be done in a minute. I have an idea for you."

Sophie sat in the window, eating her cookies. She was calm now, sitting here waiting for Brenda. She was lucky to have found her.

When Brenda came through the checkout counter, she said, "Put your suitcase in the bottom of the cart." She had the groceries and the kids in the basket. "We'll wheel it home. This place I'm going to show you, it's in my building. You're not afraid of a little hard work, are you?"

Sophie helped push the wagon up the hill. Jessie put her hand on Sophie's hand.

"Take your hand off Sophie!" Brenda said.

"No," Sophie said. "She can leave it there."

"She's going to get you dirty."

"I'm used to it," Sophie said.

"Good. Let me tell you about this place. It's no palace. The people who lived there before were pigs. Wait'll you see the bathtub. The crud is an inch thick. Unbelievable. I don't think they ever cleaned it, and the landlord, he'll never do it. He asked me to do it. I said no way. I mop the halls and I take out the garbage, and he gives me a break on my rent, but I'm not cleaning other people's filth. But if you want it, you can probably get it cheap."

Brenda's building was off the street. A paved parking lot separated it from a tall apartment house. Brenda unlocked the outside door, then went and got the keys for the empty apartment. It was on the second floor, two rooms and a windowless bath, plus a tiny kitchen. It was filthy, littered with papers and garbage, a layer of grease and grime over everything. The windows were so dirty Sophie couldn't see out. The first thing she did was throw open a window.

What she liked immediately was the tree outside the window, its trunk scarred from hooks and clothesline pulleys. The sticky, fat buds were just beginning to open. It made her feel at home. "I'll take it," she said. The cleanup didn't scare her.

"Let me call the landlord. He'll want a month's rent in advance."

"I don't have a job yet. Do you think he'll take a down payment?"

"When I tell him you're going to clean this dump up . . . that's worth more than a month's rent. He ought to pay you. I'm going to tell him that. You hold on to your money till you get a job. Maybe my husband'll have an idea. Martin drives a cab, so he hears about a lot of stuff. And I'll tell the landlord he's got to pay for the paint if he wants you to paint this place. Whatever you do, you're doing him a favor, don't forget that."

After Brenda settled things with the landlord, she lent Sophie a broom, a mop and a pail, and a box of cleanser. Sophie left her suitcase downstairs in Brenda's apartment and went to work. It took her a couple of hours just to carry out all the garbage. Then she washed the windows and scraped the grease off the sills. She brought her suitcase up and put her little china animals on the clean sills and tried to imagine where she would set plants and where she would put a table and chairs. She started to feel happy.

Brenda invited her to supper. While Brenda cooked, Sophie bathed the baby, Violet, and fed her. Martin, Brenda's husband, said he thought Sophie ought to try for a job in a store or a factory. He was a skinny man with a long neck and a gimpy leg.

"She lived on a farm," Brenda said. "She likes the outdoors."

"Where's she going to get a job outside? Girls work inside, in stores and offices and that sort of place."

"Not every single one," Brenda said. "There's got to be one exception. There's got to be one girl who's working outside."

"Yeah, crossing guards by schools."

"That's no money. What about construction? I see girls working there."

"Politics. You've got to know somebody."

That night Sophie wrapped up in a couple of blankets that Brenda lent her and slept on the floor in her apartment. Light came in from the street. She rolled her jacket for a pillow and lay on her back. She saw her tree, heard traffic noises, sometimes a siren in the distance. At moments she heard the wind, then voices inside the house.

For almost her whole life she'd slept in the same room, at the head of the stairs in her parents' house. She knew every crack on the walls, every stain on the ceiling, the way the light came through the windows, and in spring how the lilac bush shadowed her whole room.

She turned one way and then the other. She didn't think she'd ever fall asleep or get used to all these sounds. The things that had happened to her today kept passing through her mind. This morning she had been on the farm and now she was here.

She dozed off, but woke when she heard voices again. A man and a woman were arguing. It sounded like they were in the apartment with her. The woman yelled. There were footsteps, things falling. The woman's voice went on and on. A door slammed and then it slammed again.

Sophie thought of the farm, of the sky, of the silence of the night, and the way all the sounds blended together—the wind, the animals, the pigeons under the eaves. Night sounds that spread over her like a blanket. Sometimes Jupiter barked at a skunk nosing in the grass. But in the morning he was always on her bed, lying across her legs. She missed his weight now.

Six

It was dark that day when Willis got home from work. The shades were still down from the morning. The dog was lying in the bathtub on its side, almost exactly as he'd left it in the morning. It didn't look like a dog at all. It looked like a piece of fur somebody had tossed aside. It was only when Willis knelt down that he saw its side fluttering.

The dog opened its eyes, raised its head, tried to move toward him. Its eyes closed and then opened again. Willis watched the dog for a while. It was a she. A female. Her helplessness made him remember the nights he'd sat watching his father, sitting against the wall, too drunk to stand and too drunk to sleep.

What had he gotten himself into with this dog? He didn't want her. His mother had never allowed a dog into their apartment. She had his father. That was enough trouble. Willis didn't need trouble, either.

"What're you going to do?" he asked the dog. "Are

you going to die? If you're going to die, I'm taking you back where I found you. You can't die here." The dog just lay there. She looked like something dead already. It made him angry. "Get up. Come on! Or I'm taking you back."

He got a hand under the dog and propped her up. "Now you look like a dog. Stay that way." But the moment he took his hand away, the dog sagged down again.

What a mess. He'd made a stupid mistake, bringing home a dying dog. People would laugh if they knew. He'd really let himself be suckered by this poor, big-eyed puppy stuff.

In the kitchen, he ate a piece of cold pizza. He poured some of his soda into a saucer and shared it with the dog. She managed to lap some of it up. Then she was down again, and her eyes shut. Her tail moved once. The rest of her looked dead again. He covered her with newspaper. Tomorrow, he'd get rid of her.

He washed up and went out. On the corner there was a pizza joint that he liked. It was a family place, where he could sit and watch TV while he ate. He ordered a plate of ravioli, then flipped channels till he found a sports program, replays of great moments in sports history.

He shook cheese on his ravioli and watched the race between Zola Budd and Mary Decker. The schoolgirl and the veteran. Zola was another barefooted runner like Aaron Hill. Willis was for Zola, the newcomer, the underdog, the come-from-behind challenger. Mary Decker had had her day—now it was Zola's time.

When Zola took the lead, Willis had his face right up against the TV. "Hold that inside position. Hold it, Zola!" Mary Decker was crowding her. "Don't give way, Zola! Go! Go! Go!"

For a while they ran stride for stride, and then—even knowing it was coming he couldn't believe it when it happened. First, the two runners, shoulder to shoulder, moving with the precision of geared wheels, and then chaos. Mary going down, Zola fighting to keep her balance. Zola ran on, but you could tell the heart was out of her. Willis didn't want her to give up. "It's not your fault, Zola. Go! Run! Win!"

In the middle of the night the dog started whimpering and woke him. He staggered into the bathroom and brought her some water. Toward morning, he dreamed about Zola Budd. They were training together, both of them running barefoot, bare shoulder to bare shoulder, her stride matching his stride, step for step, so smooth they hardly touched the ground. The two of them flowing on and on, their heels rising and falling, light as Ping-Pong balls.

The next day at work, he was tired. He stayed out of the foreman's way, but Miholic came looking for him. He had a job for Willis on the shipping platform. "I want you to neat up the joint, Pierce. Stack the skids. Sweep up. Get this place so we can see the floor again."

Willis got the broom and shovel and went to work. He moved the big stuff off the floor first, the boxes, pallets and lumber. His mind was on the work mostly, but he noticed that every time the air compressor kicked off and its steady, regular rhythm stopped, he thought of the dog.

A couple of the older guys on the floor, Vinnie and Wolpe, weren't doing much of anything but watching him horse the pallets around. "Hey, kid, come here." Wolpe motioned him over. "Slow down." Wolpe had a square, hard face that looked like it was spattered with pepper.

"Take it easy, kid. You don't have to move that stuff by hand. Wait for the lift truck."

Willis pulled a steel bin around, then started sweeping. Vinnie and Wolpe were a couple of pals, old crows who had been at Consolidated forever. They liked ordering Willis around, telling him he was doing things wrong. They wanted him to know that he was new and they had more rank than he did.

Vinnie, who had a sad, fat face, took the broom. "Like this, Willis. Nice, easy strokes. In between you rest and look around. You don't strain your heart. If you don't see the big man, you rest some more."

"And when we get to the heavy stuff," Wolpe said, "we have a long-range point of view. We think of our backs. We think of the future. We think about who's going to hire us if we break our backs. We get the forklift. We call Benny over."

When they gave him advice, he listened. You had to listen. When he first came here, he hoped he'd find a friend, a guy he'd stand with before the whistle blew. They could talk about what they'd seen the night before on TV and eat lunch together and share the newspaper. They'd laugh about Wolpe and Vinnie and say what a royal pain the two of them were.

"Will-ass!" Wolpe had a voice like sandpaper. "I told you to take it easy. You're killing the job. Get Benny over here."

Benny Rinaldi was sitting nearby on the lift truck looking bored. He was around Willis's age, a smooth-looking guy, hair combed back, and dark, shiny eyes.

"Move the bin, Rinaldi," Wolpe yelled.

Benny started up the lift truck. Willis guided the forks

under the bin. Benny nodded, lifted the bin and drove off.

Lunchtime Willis sat on a pail at the edge of the loading dock. He ate slowly and took his time reading the newspaper. Occasionally he'd look up to see what was happening. The younger guys were by the overhead doors. Benny Rinaldi was standing up, gesturing and talking, telling dirty jokes.

Willis turned to the sports page and read about the Big Peanut Run down in Atlanta, Georgia. A half marathon. He never read about a race without imagining himself in it. Which was odd, because he never competed. His choice.

In the inside section there was a picture of a dog who had found its way home across thirteen states. The picture showed the dog reunited with its owners, a man and a woman, the dog between them. The dog looked happy. Not like the dog he'd found. Nobody was waiting for that poor sucker.

After lunch, Miholic sent Willis and Benny over to TR Two, where the women worked, to crate up a machine and get it ready for shipping. When Willis and Benny appeared there was a lot of head turning and calls and whistles. Benny rolled his shoulders. The attention was all for him. Willis thought Benny looked like a movie star.

The machine they had to crate was a monster. They had to build a box around it, tie it and brace it. They worked with framing lumber, steel bands and cinching pliers. They didn't talk a lot. They worked well together, fast and clean.

When they had the machine boxed and crated, Willis signaled for the overhead crane. The crane operator waved her scarf. Benny nudged him. "She's got her eye on you, man."

Willis and Benny grabbed opposite pairs of chains and hooked them to the four corners of the crate. Willis signaled the crane operator to take it away. She tooted as the crane went screeching down the bay.

They killed some time hanging around the Coke machine. It was too early to go back. "You see that girl over there?" Benny nodded toward the assemblers. "The one with the big hoop earrings? I know her. You want me to fix you up with her?"

"Why don't you fix yourself up with her?"

"I've got more than I can handle, man. Look, I'm not kidding. Just say the word."

When guys started talking about girls and women, Willis was on guard, not knowing what to expect or believe, afraid they were waiting for him to talk about the women in his life.

Confession: He didn't have a girlfriend, had barely talked to a girl since he left high school. He'd gone out with one girl in junior high, Sue Tyson, but that was so long ago it didn't count.

"How about her?" Benny pointed to a shiny-faced girl in a pair of belted coveralls.

"You know anything about dogs?" Willis said.

"My mother knows a lot about dogs. She raises toy terriers."

"This is a no-breed dog. A sick dog."

"Shoot it." Benny said cheerfully.

Willis finished his soda. "You want another?"

"You buying? Sure. You want to see a picture of my girlfriend?"

"Not especially."

"You know, you're a funny guy." Benny wiped his hands carefully, then pulled out a packet of plastic-covered photos from his shirt pocket. "This is Lee, my girlfriend. I love this girl." He handed a photo to Willis, holding it by the edges like it was a precious record. "Careful. Let me see your hands. These are professional photos."

In every photo, Lee was on a bed, either sitting up or lying down, or leaning on one elbow. In some shots she wore a nightie, in others it could have been a bikini, but Willis had a feeling it was her underwear. Willis had never seen pictures like these outside of magazines. They weren't exactly dirty, but they weren't the kind of photo passed around the family, either.

"They call that boudoir art," Benny said. "We had those taken specially."

Willis went through the photos fast, then handed them back.

"So what do you think?" Benny said. "Isn't she gorgeous?"

What did Benny want him to say? "She's your girlfriend?"

"She sure is." Benny kissed the photo. "She's the greatest girl in the world."

Willis couldn't figure Benny out. What was he showing him those pictures for? If you had a girlfriend, that was something private. If Lee were his girlfriend, he sure wouldn't show her half dressed this way.

Benny took a cigarette and offered Willis the pack.

"I run," Willis said.

Benny lit up and inhaled deeply. "I'll tell you the truth, man. Even with Lee, I envy you single guys. All those girls. All the good times. Once you get a steady girlfriend, that's all over, man. Lee keeps me on a short leash. No more roaming the range. She says look, but don't touch. Sometimes I think I should have stayed single. You're smart, man. You think, keep things close. I observed that about you. You're a deep thinker. That's a plus, man, you know what I mean?" Benny leaned close to Willis. It was noisy and he was talking into Willis's ear. "You have a girlfriend, Willis?"

"No, I have a dog."

"Ah, your sick dog. You two going steady?" Benny laughed. "I never know if you're joking or serious."

"Serious," Willis said, and got another laugh out of Benny.

Sophie left her jacket at an empty table by the window of the diner and went to wash. Handling newspapers and money all morning had blackened her fingers.

When Martin had told her there might be an outdoor job on Spring Street, Sophie had gotten really excited. She imagined an old-fashioned street with green lawns and flowering trees. The old part was right. Spring Street was just off East Broadway in the oldest part of the city. There were still stepping blocks on the curbs and cast-iron posts for tethering horses. Once, there must have been orchards and farms here, but now it was just a short, dirty street lined with a sub shop and Wallman's Army-Navy Store and a jewelry store, a unisex barber shop and four bars. Just opposite the diner, in the middle of the block, was Carl's newsstand.

That's where Sophie worked. Carl had hired her this morning and put her right to work. From the newsstand, she could see the long gray factory sheds at the end of the street. The first couple of hours she didn't think she would last. The pace! The people rushing at her, demanding papers, magazines, cigarettes, change. Hands grabbing newspapers, hands thrust out with money, hands waiting for change.

"What can I do for you, young lady?" George, the counterman, was waiting for Sophie to make a decision.

She looked up at the menu board. "Vegetable soup and a corn muffin."

"And what else?"

The chocolate cake made her mouth water. Too rich. "Do you have anything else?"

George indicated a tray of dark, sweet-looking cakes near her. "Baklava," he said. "Honey and nuts rolled in a thin dough. My wife makes them."

"I'll try one." She felt self-conscious as she walked back to the table. The place was full of men. A man was sitting at her table, and her jacket was on the floor. She picked it up and looked around for another table. They were all taken, and she sat down. "Crowded," she said. The man nodded. She took a spoonful of her soup and buttered her corn muffin. It didn't seem right to sit at a table with another person and not talk. "Enjoying your lunch?" she said.

"Um-hum."

"You left your cole slaw. I don't like cabbage, either."

The man was looking at her. "You new around here?"

"I work over there," she said proudly, pointing to the stand. "This is my first day. That man with the bald head is my boss."

"Uh-huh." He went back to eating.

She had never thought of herself as a talker, but here she was, talking a mile a minute. When had she ever talked like this before? Maybe on the farm. She'd always talked to the animals.

It gave her a pang to think of the animals and the farm and her brother—her rotten brother. He was coming into the house about now for his lunch and kicking off his boots and looking at the mail. Was he thinking about her? Not likely. He and Pat had the farm to themselves now. That gave Sophie another pang. Everything she loved was back there.

She glanced at the man next to her. She couldn't get comfortable. How could that large man sit there and eat so easily? She had to eat with one hand in her lap. She felt pinned against the wall. The table, the chair, the space she was backed into, everything seemed scaled to people half her size.

On the farm it was good to be big. Her strength counted for something. She was big across the shoulders, her arms and legs were firm and round, and she was agile getting up ladders and jumping off wagons. She wasn't clumsy. She didn't fall. She didn't hurt herself.

But here, it seemed as if she was always stumbling, running into things, bumping into people, getting hard looks. She kept having to draw herself in, suck in her breath, apologize. It was as if her body wanted to go one way and the city wanted her to go another.

From the diner window, she saw Carl outside the stand, arranging the magazines. He had a bald head and dark glasses. He had stayed with her all morning, but starting tomorrow, she was on her own. The first thing he told her this morning was how busy he was. He had newspaper stands and a newspaper delivery franchise, plus houses he rented out.

"I have to have someone dependable at the stand," he said. "Someone who can take charge and likes getting up early and isn't afraid of hard work." He showed her how he wanted her to lock up at the end of the day, then he handed her the key. "Don't lose it." She put it on her key chain. Now she had a key for the newsstand, a key for the outside door of her house, one for the mailbox and two keys to open the door to her apartment. Nothing was ever locked on the farm.

"And you'll be here at six on the dot tomorrow morning? If you're going to stay up all night with your boyfriend, you'll be too tired. Tell him you'll see him on the weekend."

"I don't have a boyfriend."

"Good. Remember, the papers are always here at six. You gotta be here or they'll steal you blind. I'm counting on you, Sophie."

At the end of the day, she took her time going home. It was warm and she carried her jacket over her arm. She was hardly tired. You had to pay attention when you were selling newspapers, but it wasn't like farm work. The wind blustered and blew. It was a playful wind that pushed her from behind, then caught her as she rounded the corner.

As she continued up East Broadway there were buildings and the sky opened up. She saw a small plane flying low overhead. She stopped and watched it until it disappeared. She saw the plane, but the people in it couldn't see her. Up there, they saw something else. They saw the city and past the city to the horizon and beyond the horizon.

That was part of the free feeling she had when she flew. The world was bigger up there, bigger than she had ever imagined. It was the same feeling she got when she looked at the stars at night. In one way it made you feel smaller, because you were just a little part of all that, but in another way it made you feel bigger and freer—and happier.

Eight

Near the tunnel entrance to the plant, Willis grabbed his usual paper at the newsstand. The new girl was alone this morning and slower than molasses. He handed her a ten-dollar bill and she was stymied. She was looking at her hands; her lips were moving. "Just give me nine dollars and seventy-five cents," he said.

"I know that."

"So what's the problem? You think the ten is counterfeit?"

She gave him a dumb smile. "I don't know if I can make that much change. I mean, I can make it, but I might need it for later. Do you have anything smaller?"

"No."

She handed him back his money. He tossed the paper back. "No, take it," she said. "You can pay me later."

"Later? What makes you think I'll pay you?"

"Oh, you will." Her face broke out in a smile. She trusted him. He grabbed the paper and ran.

Later, when he went by, he had the quarter ready, but she was gone. So she was wrong, he didn't pay her.

That night he made supper for himself and hand-fed the dog a scrambled egg. This was her third day with him. He never thought she'd last this long. Now that she was feeling better, he could see she was a pretty dog, with a pointed, foxy-looking muzzle and white eyebrows. White markings on her legs, too, like stockings.

He'd called his mother the night before last to ask what to feed somebody who was sick. "Who?" she said. "Who is this person?"

"Did I say it was a person, Mom? It could be a cat or a dog."

"Okay, this person, this cat, what's she got?"

"She's not feeling good. She's kind of beat up."

"Beat up? What kind of girl is she?"

"Did I say she was a girl?"

"Where'd you meet her?"

"Mom, what should I feed her? She's really weak. She needs to build up her strength." He didn't want to say he had a dog in the house, a sick dog. His mother didn't like dogs.

"You didn't meet her in a bar, did you?"

"Ma. Me in a bar? Are you kidding? This is your son you're talking to."

"Egg," his mother said. "For someone weak, soft things that are easy to digest. Milk, soft bread, toast and rice, well-cooked, nice and soft." And then, just before she hung up, she said, "Am I going to meet her? You know, we're coming this summer."

"If she's still around, you'll meet her."

He opened a jar of baby vegetables, made a mash of it

with the egg. Disgusting-looking stuff. He squatted down next to the dog. "Now eat."

When she finished eating, he rubbed olive oil on her swollen legs, then poured it right over the wounds. It was his father's remedy. Olive oil in your salad, olive oil on your skin, olive oil for whatever ailed you.

"So when are you going to start walking, Zola?" The name just popped out. Zola, after Zola Budd. Maybe the name would help her run again. "If you run a tenth as good as Zola Budd, you'll be a great dog."

In the middle of the night, the dog crept over to his mattress and started whining. "What do you want?" He was only half awake and pulled her up next to him. In the morning she was there, curled up behind his knees. "You're not exactly the girl of my dreams," he told her.

The next day at work, he checked the phone book and found the address of a veterinarian on Central Avenue. When he got home, he wrapped Zola in a blanket and took her to the vet. Every seat in Dr. Goldman's waiting room was taken. Across the room, a Doberman sat watching him alertly. A woman was holding a Persian cat, and sitting next to her was a man holding two sleek, blue-eyed Siamese. Willis felt like he and Zola were a couple of mongrels.

"Can I help you?" the receptionist asked. She was wearing glasses with tiny little cats etched on the lenses. "Your appointment?"

"I don't have one."

"Oh, you need an appointment."

"My dog is really sick."

"May I see her?" She raised a corner of the blanket. "Oh, the poor thing."

He started to explain. "Somebody—"

"What's her name?"

"Zola."

"Zola? Is that a first name or a last name?"

"First name."

"Last name?"

"Mine or the dog's?"

"Yours will do."

"Pierce."

"Zola Pierce. Sit down," she said. "Doctor will see you soon."

Dr. Goldman was tall, with bright round eyes and a bushy, ginger-colored mustache. He examined Zola on a stainless steel table. Back here, the dog smell was stronger and the dog chorus was louder. Willis kept patting Zola, who cowered on the table.

The doctor looked into her eyes, then listened to her heart. He examined her legs carefully. Zola winced a couple of times, but she didn't cry. "Sorry, pet," the doctor said, "this will only take a moment more. How did this happen?"

"She was tied with wire. Somebody threw her away to die."

The doctor sighed and rubbed Zola's head.

"Is she going to be all right? Is she going to walk?"

"She's young. That's on her side, but her legs are badly infected. I'm going to give her an injection, and there are some antibiotics I want you to give her orally. No broken bones, but these two back legs, the muscles and tendons are in bad shape. You better bring her in again in a couple of weeks and let me have another look at her."

On their way out, Willis made another appointment and paid the bill. It took all the money he had, including the ten-dollar bill the news girl had handed back to him. Zola squirmed out from under the blanket and licked his ear.

"Yeah, you've got a lot of appreciation, but that don't pay the bills."

Nine

Sophie saw the fellow she'd given the paper to going past the stand a couple of times. He'd paid her, but since then he hadn't stopped. She was disappointed. She kept on noticing him, which was funny because she saw so many men every day. It was perverse of her the way she kept noticing this one guy. He wasn't tall, but he wasn't short, either. He was wide in the shoulders, narrow in the hips. He was always beltless, wearing the same checked flannel shirt and a funny white cap. Oh, she really gave him a good looking-over. She liked the way he held himself—lightly, even gracefully. He had a nice face, too, frowning slightly—a nice, worried face.

Brenda's husband, Martin, had a funny face, his teeth were stained and he had a limp. He sometimes drove Sophie to work. "Give you a ride anytime I'm on my way to work, Brownie."

Sitting next to him in the car, she'd play a little game, imagine she was Brenda and married to Martin and he was driving her to work. But it was hard to believe, because he was so much older.

Brenda had her own car, an old rusted-out Chevy. She was trying to build up a door-to-door cosmetics business. Since Sophie had moved in, she'd been leaving Jessie with her and taking the baby, strapped in the car seat. Jessie always tried to get into the car with her mother. She fought to the last minute. Sophie would hold her, whisper in her ear. "It's okay, Jessie. We'll have fun. More fun than you do with Mommy."

Brenda started the car. "Jessie, shut up and listen. You be good with Sophie, or else."

"Go on, Brenda, go on. We can take care of ourselves. I'll take care of her."

"Martin's sleeping, Soph, so try to keep her away from the house."

The minute Brenda was out of sight, Jessie stopped fighting and took Sophie's hand, and they went for a walk. They stopped at a Woolworth's, and Sophie bought Jessie a pink comb and some ribbons and got herself a potholder shaped like an owl and another plant. She bought a plant almost every day.

When they got home, Brenda still wasn't back, so Sophie brought Jessie up to her apartment. Sophie put the new geranium on the kitchen windowsill, then pinched and cleaned her other plants. She had too many plants, but she couldn't stop buying them. She got up on a chair to spray the big Boston fern she'd bought last week. A big green bushy bear that she couldn't resist. She pushed her face into its dampness. "It's pretty, isn't it?" she said to Jessie.

Jessie grabbed one of Sophie's china horses. "Be careful," Sophie said, jumping down. "We have to be nice to the horse. Put him on the floor, now move him around. Don't throw him! You know what he says? Horse says *neeeiiiiggghhh*!"

Sophie enjoyed having Jessie to take care of. A lot of times, though, she had nothing to do when she came home from work, not even a walk with Jessie. She'd eat, thinking about the day. She was settling in on the job. Her accounts were coming out right. She'd been off by only ten cents today. A few days ago, she'd been short ten dollars and had made it up out of her own pocket. Her mind switched to the fellow with the ten-dollar bill. White Cap. Was he married? He seemed too young, but he probably had a girlfriend.

After she cleaned up her dishes, she didn't know what to do with herself. She'd find herself thinking about the farm and her brother and Pat. And that got her nowhere. When she couldn't stand being alone anymore, she'd go down the stairs and stand in front of Brenda's door, listening to the voices from inside the apartment. But then she'd go on by. Brenda had a family. She didn't need Sophie hanging around there every minute.

She went out walking, went where there were people. To the playground, where she liked to get on the swing and soar, whip it up. Not exactly flying, but it had to do for now. She was trying to save money, but everything was so expensive. Lessons were twice as much as they were at home. But just that little bit of a lift on the swing, getting up above the fence and looking over the low roofs, gave her a great feeling.

She liked to walk on East Broadway, where all the stores were. And she liked the quiet side streets, too, where the houses stood one next to the other. If she saw a house she liked, one with a little green around it, she imagined that she lived there and that as she went by, the door would open and *he* would come out. The *he* she used to dream about had been faceless. But now she let herself imagine the guy with the ten-dollar bill. White Cap. It would be him standing at the door, and when he saw her, he'd wave and call her over. And she'd go in with him.

That night, before she went to sleep, she made herself some cocoa. While it was heating, she moved her newest plant around to various parts of the room. It took a while to find exactly the right place for each plant. Each one had a personality; each one needed its own special place. She finally brought it back to the table, then sat there, melting a cookie in the cocoa and staring at the still-closed flowers.

Ten

The wind was blowing as Willis left for work. It grabbed his cap, and he almost lost it. A storm was coming, maybe a hurricane. A garbage can went bouncing down the street. He saw the news girl closing up her stand. A big gust of wind got under the shutter she was letting down and tore it out of her hands. It flew up, then came down on her.

"Did that hit you?"

She was holding her hand and leaning against the shutter.

"You okay?" he said. She looked down, chewing on her lip. Then he saw blood dripping from her hands. "Hey, you are hurt." There was a dazed look on her face. "Listen, you better sit down."

He caught her as her knees buckled. She was heavier than he expected. He had to grab her around the waist. She smelled like chewing gum and fresh, unlit cigarettes. He helped her over to one of the high stone steps. "Sit down. Put your head down."

"I'm all right."
"Let me see your hand."
"It's nothing," she said, but her hand was a mess. The edge of the shutter had cut her across the palm like a knife.
"Have you got a tissue?" She shook her head.
"Stay here. I'll be right back." He ran across the street to the diner. The chairs were up and George was mopping the floor. "Have you got a first-aid kit?" Willis said. "The girl at the newsstand hurt her hand." George went off to get the kit, and Willis grabbed some paper napkins and ran back.
She looked up at him as he came back, as if she'd been waiting for him. Strange look. "Are you in pain?" She shook her head. The way she was looking at him made him uncomfortable. "Give me your hand." He cleaned up the blood, then told her to hold the napkins against the wound. "Make a fist—it'll stop the bleeding."
"I hate getting cut," she said.
"I never met anyone who loved it."
She stood up. "I've got to close the stand." The shutter was banging up and down.
"Sit down. I'll do it." He went over and locked up the stand.
George, in his white apron, came across the street with warm water and a first-aid kit. "So what happened to you, young lady?" he said.
"Oh! Look at the attention I'm getting. You look like a doctor," she said to George. She was talking all of a sudden. "You want to see it?"
"Don't show it to me. I'm no good around blood." He handed Willis the first-aid kit. "I'm always cutting my fingers in the kitchen. Look at these scars." He held out

his hand. "That's what happens when you work around food. You see that little finger? I lost the tip of it shredding cabbage."

"Oh!" she said. "That's awful. Oh, how terrible."

The two of them were carrying on with each other like a couple of patients in an emergency room. "Here, give me that," Willis said. He took the first-aid kit, found a sterile pad and bandages. "Hold out your hand," he told the girl.

"Okay, you're in charge." George went back to the diner.

"I'm Sophie Browne," the girl said, like they were at a tea party. "I appreciate . . . what's your name?"

"Willis Pierce." He washed around the wound.

"Do you think I'll need stitches, Willis?"

He broke out a roll of gauze, tore open the seals, then bandaged her hand. He liked the way she was looking at him. "A cut like that should heal right up." He sounded very professional. "How's that feel?"

"It looks like a boxing glove. Do you work on an ambulance or something?"

"No, I work over in Consolidated. Is it too tight?"

"I don't feel anything."

"You will tomorrow. You'd better see a doctor. Tell your boss he's got to pay for it."

"He won't like it."

"Tough. It's not your fault. You got hurt on the job, that's all you have to tell him. If you need a witness, call me."

She stood up.

"How do you feel? Are you dizzy?"

"No, I'm fine. Thanks. Thanks very much . . . Willis Pierce."

That would have been the end of it. It should have been the end, but something about the way she said his name got to him. He liked the way she said it. Willis Pierce. She said his name as if she liked the sound of it, maybe liked him. "Wait a minute." He held up the first-aid kit. "Wait till I bring this back to George."

He walked with her to the bus, the wind at their backs. They didn't really say that much to each other. "How's that hand doing?" he said.

"Oh, fine, Willis. You did a great job. You really fixed it."

"This is only my first house call." He told her about Zola.

"Somebody tied wires around her legs? Who would be that mean?"

"Are you kidding? You sell the papers. Don't you read them?"

"Well, yes, but newspapers . . ."

"It's not just the papers. Lousy things happen everywhere."

She was silent for a moment. "I guess I don't want to really believe things are that awful."

There was a bench by the bus stop. "Sit down," he said. "Feeling better?"

"It's beginning to hurt."

"These things hurt for a while, then they feel better." He showed her the scars on his hands and wrists. "George isn't the only one with scars. You see this one?" he said, pointing to a crooked scar down the length of his thumb. "I got that when I was seven years old. They gave me seven stitches, that's how I remember. And this one?" He touched a raised scar over his eyebrow. "My old man kissed me there once."

"He kissed you?"

"With his fist."

"He hit you?"

"He didn't know he had his ring on." He was sorry he'd said anything. He never told anyone about his father. Why was he telling her? Who was she, anyway? He saw his bus on the other side of the street. "I've got to run," he said, and he left.

She sat there and let him go. You fool, Sophie Browne, she said to herself. You let him go. And then she had to laugh at herself. He was gone, but she was the one who was really gone. Gone nuts over him. That was an old-fashioned word, but that was the way she felt. Old-fashioned crazy over him.

She remembered his arms around her, her face against his face, his breath on her cheek. Her legs had gone soft and wobbly and she lay against him. Had she really been that weak? He had held her and she had let him. He had wrapped her in his arms and she hadn't struggled to get away. She'd never acted that way with anybody.

Everything about him seemed perfect. She had watched as he bandaged her hand. She had studied his face, his soft eyes and the way his ears lay against his head.

He had talked and she sat there, with the pain in her hand coming and going, not knowing if it was the pain or him, but not caring, because he was there and she didn't want to do anything to break the spell.

It had happened just like that. She was head over heels. Love at first sight. Was that it? Was that the way it happened? Was it to be believed?

Eleven

Willis took a clean shirt off the hanger and dropped it on the mattress. Zola watched him get dressed. "In an hour, in less than an hour, Zola, at ten to six exactly, I'm going to meet Benny Rinaldi and the beautiful Lee and a friend of hers. Blind date. She's got to be as gorgeous as Lee. Or does she?"

He looked for a matching pair of socks, then put on his sneakers. "I'm looking forward to it, Zola. That makes me a fool. I'm hoping. I can't help it. Because I'm a fool."

Before he left, he opened a can of baby food and spooned some into Zola's dish. He put the dish in front of her, a little out of her reach, so she had to pull herself over to it.

"That's it. Reach, baby."

He still couldn't get over the way Zola had popped into his life. What if he hadn't taken that shortcut? What if he hadn't stopped? What if he hadn't gone down to the water and checked out the plastic bag? Chances were a million to one that she'd be dead right now. And, looking at her, watching her lap up the food, that seemed impossible.

The newsstand girl popped into his mind. Another jack-in-the-box. Another accident in his life. He saw her almost every day. Since the night she'd hurt herself, he'd been waving to her on his way to work. He waved, she waved. He stopped once, asked how her hand was. Just a moment, then he rushed on, and he didn't stop again. She wanted him to stop. She didn't say it, but he knew.

He dropped a couple of pills into Zola's bowl, then put some water in her cup. She pulled herself around on her front legs. "Maybe you'll be one of those dogs that walks on its front paws. And you'll be in a circus and make a lot of money and forget me. Yes, you're smiling now, but when you're famous you'll say, Willis? Who's he?"

He studied himself in the bathroom mirror. Get that worried look off your face. Stop worrying! Smile! Look relaxed and confident. What can she do to you? Let's think about that. Squeeze you to death? Tear your clothes off? Anytime.

He combed his hair forward, then to one side. He hung some gold around his neck and left his shirt unbuttoned. "How's that, Zola? Dazzling?"

He looked at himself again. Uh-uh, too cute. He changed, put on his old, faded, running suit. "That's the way I'm going, Zola." He got down and whispered in her ear. "I'm nervous enough." He grabbed his Raleigh racing cap, pulled it down over one eye, then reversed it, but finally set it square on his head. "Zola! Tell you all about it when I see you later."

Benny and the two girls were waiting for him outside the Fourplex at Shopping Town. Benny was wearing a leather jacket and a black turtleneck and a lot of gold around his neck. "Willis, this is Lee. And this"—he made like a bugle—"is Dore, *ta da!* Dore and Lee, this is Willis Pierce, my buddy from work. No, don't worry about it," he said, as Willis reached for his money. He had his arm around Willis and grabbed Willis's cap. "Do you sleep in that thing?"

Willis glanced at Dore, looked longer at Lee, then couldn't stop looking at her. She was as beautiful as the photos Benny had showed him. No, better. She could have been a model. A lot of beautiful hair and big, gorgeous, dark eyes.

Her friend Dore was pretty, too. He gave her a smile. She and Lee were both wearing tight pants and heels. Dore had on some kind of a feathery pink blouse. She liked pink. She had pink nails and pink lipstick.

"You must be a runner," Lee said to him.

"I run every day."

"That's wonderful."

"That's the main thing I do. Besides work. I run before I work." He looked down at his wrinkled sneakers.

"Did you hear that, Benny? Look at the shape Willis is in. And look at you." Lee patted Benny's gut. "Dore, Willis runs every day and what do we do?"

"I run," Dore said.

"Like a ten-wheel truck," Benny said.

Dore punched him. "I do not. What did you say something like that for?"

Benny limped around, holding his shoulder as if she'd hurt him. "Tell us about it, Dore. These two women drive me crazy," he said happily to Willis. He stood between the two girls, his arms draped over their shoulders.

Willis felt he should say something to Dore. "You don't run in those high heels, do you?"

"I have enough trouble walking in them."

"I noticed," Benny said. "You wobble a lot." That got him another punch.

Inside, Willis went around to Dore's side. "Popcorn?" he asked. He went to the candy stand, telling himself the important thing was to talk, stay loose, not freeze up. He was part of this group, too. They were all together. He bought two tubs of popcorn, one for Benny and Lee, one for Dore and him.

As they walked into the theater, Benny said, "Matched you up perfectly, didn't I?"

Inside, the two girls sat in the middle, the two boys on the outside. Willis held the popcorn out to Dore.

"No, thanks. They stick in my teeth."

He took a handful. "You go to the movies a lot?"

"I love the movies." She touched her earrings.

He put his arm across the back of her seat. Her earrings were like little pink candies. "What have you seen lately?"

She turned to Lee and Benny. "What movie have I seen lately?"

It was hard to keep a conversation going because her head kept turning to the others. He'd say something. She'd look at him, she'd answer, and then she'd turn back to Lee and Benny.

"Do you run a lot?" he said.

"Not much." She turned to Lee.

"I don't feel normal if I don't run every day."

"Uh-huh." Still looking at Lee.

"Running makes me feel good. It makes anybody who does it feel good."

"So I hear." She reached across Lee and tapped Benny. "Right, fatso?"

Willis was ready to like Dore. That was the whole idea.

He kept trying. "Running does something good to your brain." He felt like he was talking to the back of her head. "You ever hear of endorphins? It's a natural high. Better than drugs. Cheaper, too. You ever hear of Aaron Hill?"

"No." She looked around briefly. "I run when I feel fat," she said.

"You don't look fat to me."

That got a smile out of her. As it happened, that was the high point of the evening.

After a while, he took his arm away and sat dipping into the tub of popcorn between them and watching the people still coming into the theater.

The movie was about college kids, a boy watching a girl and getting rebuffed. Willis identified with the boy. Just like him and Dore. Sometimes he imagined himself in college. The only way he'd ever get there would be on an athletic scholarship. A runner. They'd say about him that no miler like him had come along since Aaron Hill at Villanova. The girls wouldn't be running away from him, either.

He often wondered what would've happened if he'd done things differently. What if he'd gone out for the track team in high school? Would he be in college now? He should have been on the high school track team. But in junior high he'd run in a school race once, and it had been a disaster.

His father had come to see him, but he'd been drunk and had run out on the field, cheering for Willis. The thought of it, even now, knotted Willis up. He'd never run in a race again.

After the movie, the four of them stood outside the theater, trying to decide what they were going to do next. "Let's go bowling," Lee said.

"You want me to break my fingernails off?" Dore showed her long pink nails. "I just spent an hour putting them on."

"How about roller skating, then?"

"Not me," Benny said.

Willis stretched out.

"How about you, Willis? Any bright ideas?" Lee said.

He looked at her. Just being near her made him weak through the middle. Oh, god, he felt like he was in junior high. She was waiting for him to say something. "Let's all go out for a run."

Dore snorted. "Sure. In my high heels."

"I think it's a nice idea," Lee said quickly. "It's something different, anyway."

"Lee," Dore said, "did you hear Chuck's latest moron joke?"

"Who's Chuck?" Willis said.

"The store manager at Fairview, where Lee and I work," Dore said, as if anyone with half a brain would've known that.

"I'm a cashier," Lee said, "but Dore is a big cheese."

Dore and Benny groaned.

"What's the joke?" Willis said.

"The joke," Dore explained, "is I work at the cheese counter. Cheese department. Big cheese. Get it?"

Yeah. He got it.

"Now, do you want to hear a real joke? Are you ready?" Dore looked at him, really looked interested for the first time all evening. "How do you keep a moron in suspense?"

"How?" he said, and the minute he said it, he knew he'd stepped into the trap. How do you keep a moron in suspense? He was the moron, because he'd asked, and

Dore was just looking at him, and Lee and Benny were laughing.

"Willis, you fell for it."

"Funny, funny, funny." He showed his teeth. He wanted to spit something clever back. What he wouldn't have given for a comeback remark.

"Come on, you guys, let's do something," Lee said. "Let's go dancing, Benny."

"Benny doesn't like dancing," Dore said. "Anyway, my feet hurt."

"Your poor little feet," Benny said. "Let's go get something to eat."

"I knew things were going to end up that way," Lee said.

"Why don't we pick up some beer and pizza and go over to Willis's house?" Benny said.

"My house? I don't have a house. It's just one room."

"That's all we need."

"It's a mess."

"That's okay. The girls will clean it up."

"Fat chance," Lee said.

Benny kept nodding his head to Willis, sending him signals. Agree, agree, this is a great idea. "Come on," Benny said, reaching into Willis's pocket. "Where's your key, old buddy?"

He didn't want them in his house. Lee maybe, once he cleaned it up, but not Benny and Dore, looking at what he had and making jokes about it. "My dog is sick."

"You still talking about that dog? I don't think you have a dog."

"Cut it out, Benny," Lee said. "Can't you see he doesn't want to do it? Let's do something else."

They finally went for hamburgers and fries. Willis kept

watching Lee, but when she looked at him, he looked away. She was Benny's girl, but if she wasn't . . . maybe it could happen. She was paying attention to him, too. He couldn't believe how much she was like the girl he dreamed about. And she was nice. He liked everything about her—the way she looked, the way she dressed, how easy it was to talk to her. What if Dore and Benny got together? Then he and Lee could team up.

When the food came, he saved one of his hamburgers for Zola.

"Is that for later, when you get hungry?" Dore said.

He looked at her suspiciously. Why did the little moron take home a hamburger? "It's for Zola," he said.

"Who's Zola?"

"Someone I live with."

That got her attention. "Someone you live with? Well, if you live with somebody, what are you doing here?"

"She likes me to go out once in a while and have some fun."

"Oh," Dore said, and turned to make a face to the others.

Zola was waiting for him when he got home. She pulled herself to the door like a kid pulling a wagon.

"Glad I'm home, aren't you? Or is it the hamburger?" He knelt down and broke off pieces and let her take it off his hand. She kept looking at him between bites. When everything was gone, she licked his hand. He had more enthusiasm from Zola in five minutes than he had from Dore all evening.

Twelve

Saturday morning in the rain, Willis jogged over to Fairview on East Broadway to shop. That was where Lee and Dore worked. He was hoping he'd spot them. Well, not them. Lee.

Fairview was an enormous market, with eight checkouts, but no Lee. He saw Dore over in Gourmet Cheese. She wore the Fairview red jacket and a little white cap. He didn't think she saw him. Just as well. Lee was working in another department, or maybe she was on a break. He wheeled a cart around, taking his time. In the pet department, he picked out a white leather collar for Zola, to match her eyebrows.

He bought a few more things—milk, dog food, and a stack of frozen pizzas that were on special. He threw in a couple of packages of frozen bagels. He liked them with cream cheese and lettuce. At the checkout, he looked for Lee again.

Nearby, a woman was giving out free lasagna samples in little paper cups. The girl from the newsstand was there. He saw her take one cup, then another. There was something a little embarrassing about it. Willis never took samples. He didn't like people giving him things and then expecting him to buy their products.

He unloaded his cart. A moment later, someone tapped him on the shoulder. "Hello, Willis."

He glanced around. "Oh, hi!" He'd never win any Academy awards for that performance.

"Remember me, Willis?"

"Sure," he said, but he'd forgotten her name.

"Sophie Browne." She smiled, as if she knew and forgave him.

Bits of green stuff stuck to her teeth. Compared to Lee—no, how could he compare her to Lee? No cool, no makeup, no beauty. Fat mouth like a kid's. But friendly. Too friendly. She struck him as being really naive about guys. She didn't know what space meant. She came right up to him until she was practically leaning on him. And she was looking into his basket.

"Ten," she said, counting the pizzas. "You must really like pizza. How long does it take you to eat all those?"

"How's the hand?" he said.

"All healed. I kept your bandage on for three days, but then it got too dirty."

The way she said it, *your* bandage, her eyes shining at him, and all that intensity focused on him made him feel like the healer of all times.

"It healed just the way you said it would."

"That's good." Dr. Welby turned to see if the line was moving. "Is that all you're buying?" he said. She had a bag of nuts and a plant. "Why don't you go ahead of me?"

"Oh, I don't mind. My day off. I'm not going anywhere."

He made room for her in front of him, anyway.

She held out a bag of pink pistachios. "Want some?"

"Pink is not my favorite color."

"You don't eat that part." She cracked one and put the empty shell in her pocket. "What I can't stand are the ones that don't open. You can't bite them open, and if you hammer them, you just make a mess." She laughed.

Too much smile. She was all right, but she was too eager. She stood too close. She needed someone to take her aside and talk to her, tell her the facts of city life. When a girl met a guy she hardly knew, she could smile and say hi, but that was all.

"Don't you think this is a beautiful begonia?" she said.

"I don't know one plant from another."

"Every plant is different. Even two pots with the same plant. One is a little tender and shy and the next one is bushy and sort of pushy. You'd know what a nut I am about plants if you saw my place."

Was that an invitation? It sure sounded like one. If she went around inviting guys, somebody was going to accept, and she might not be too happy about that. He stacked the frozen pizzas together at one end of the counter.

"Isn't there somebody who cooks for you?" She got all red.

She was definitely making moves on him. "No, I do all the cooking. For me and Zola."

"Zola?"

"Zola's my dog," Bighearted Willis. He should have let

her wonder, but she wasn't a Dore. Still, he should have kept his mouth shut, because she was off again.

"Oh, Zola!" Her whole face opened up—she was shining, really shining. "Now I remember, Zola's your dog! You told me about her. I should have remembered, the name is so unusual. I'd love to meet her. I love dogs."

He almost laughed, she was so obvious. She wants to come up and meet Zola? She might find more than one animal living up there. Somebody ought to tell her the story of Little Red Riding Hood and the big bad wolf.

"My dog's name is Jupiter. He's a boxer," she was saying. "And before Jupiter there was Orion, and before him . . . " She was checked out and she still lingered, telling him the names of all her dogs, their connections and genealogies.

She finally left. He gave her a wave good-bye. So long, see you around. You're a nice kid, Sophie Browne, but not exactly my type.

When he left the store, she was waiting for him outside. Not just standing there, pretending to wait for the rain to let up. Waiting for him. "Hi! I thought we could walk together." No subtlety. No finesse.

"Sure," he said. What else could he say?

She did most of the talking. Now it was about her job and her boss and where she lived, and about a little kid named Jessie.

He had to admit it was flattering to have a girl so interested in him. And it was easy. He wasn't worried every moment what Sophie thought about him. He knew. Not like Dore and her little moron jokes. "I was out running this morning," he said.

"In the rain?"

"Rain or shine. It's got to be really pouring to keep me in."

"Do you run a lot?"

She gave him that shining look, and he started telling her about running. The same stuff he had tried to tell Dore, but this was completely different. Sophie was listening, the way nobody had ever listened before. Once he got started, there was no stopping him. He had a lot to say about running.

"This is my corner," he said at last. He'd meant to leave her a lot sooner.

"Where do you live?"

He pointed over his shoulder. "That way."

"Jefferson Street?"

"No."

"Central Avenue?"

"Uh-huh."

"Well, I guess I'll see you when I'm at the newsstand."

Standing there, he had an impulse to tell her things. Give her advice. She came from the country and it showed. "Listen, I want to tell you something."

"I bet you want to tell me how to get home. You're right! I don't even know where I am."

"You know, you shouldn't talk like that. What if I was some creep?"

"Willis Pierce! You're not a creep."

Okay. He gave up. "Where do you live?"

"Turner Avenue."

"You have to go back to the market," he said, "and keep going on up East Broadway."

"Just point me in the right direction. That's what my daddy used to say. Point me in the right direction and turn me loose."

He went over the directions with her again.

"I've got it. Maybe, sometime, you'll introduce me to Zola." She had this little, eager smile on her face, and then she left.

Thirteen

Sophie Browne, she said to herself, you like him too much. You waited for him, you put yourself in his way, you hung on to him. And he still didn't like you. Not enough. He didn't even remember your name.

Maybe he's just shy.

Shy? He talked, didn't he?

He's nice.

Nice? You don't know that. You don't know what he is. You don't know anything about him. Like he said, he could be a creep. You're thinking about him too much. You are. Even when you say you're not, you are. Example. Taking out the garbage. What happened?

I met Martin.

Right. And what did he say?

How you getting along, kid?

And you said, Perfect.

And he said, You meeting people?

And you said, Every day, and you gave Martin an extra big smile.

And Martin said, You've got a million-dollar smile, Brownie. He thought the smile was for him. But all the time you were talking to him, you were wishing it was Willis you'd met at the garbage, and the smile you were smiling at Martin was really a smile for Willis.

It was true. She thought about Willis all the time. Too much. Did he think about her? Then why didn't he stop at the stand once in a while? Why did he run past? Why didn't he like her when she liked him so much? What if he never liked her? Maybe he wouldn't, but she didn't want to think about it.

Every day at work, she looked for him. Even when she sold papers so fast she hardly had time to look up, she knew when he passed. She felt it, like a shiver down her back. One day she walked away from a customer, left the stand unattended to catch a glimpse of Willis's white cap disappearing down the tunnel entrance. That was bad. What if Carl had come by? She could have lost her job.

She arranged the coins in the money box, frowned at her hands. Cool down, Sophie. There's too much heat in you.

She knew it. She wanted. She wanted Willis. She didn't understand herself. She'd had crushes, had liked boys before, but never like this. She traced a finger across the scar on her palm. He'd seen her hands like this, plain and dirty, and he didn't like them. Was that it? Had he taken an instant dislike to her when he saw her hands?

Pat always wore gloves when she worked and rubbed in cream every night and took care of her nails. Those bright-red fingernails. She was always after Sophie to do something with her hands. Do what?

Her hands were her hands. She'd always worked with her hands. On the farm she wore gloves when she handled wire bails, but most of the time she couldn't wear gloves. The same with her feet. She wore sneakers or boots, or went barefoot when she wasn't working, but her feet were her feet. She didn't paint her nails. She didn't decorate herself. She was what she was.

Men liked pretty women. Pretty, cool women with clean hands and long fingernails. She wasn't pretty. Her shoulders were too broad, hips too wide, her face too plain. If she was any kind of pretty, she was un-pretty. She was herself, just Sophie.

She wasn't cool. She was eager and she said things, and sometimes people laughed at her. She laughed with them, because what difference did it make. But sometimes she wished she was cool and could remove herself and retreat into herself and look out and watch and not let anyone in. She wished she could be like the pasture pond in the first light, when everything was still and its surface was smooth as dark glass.

If she was like that, she'd watch Willis. He wouldn't know she was watching, and he'd wonder about her and he'd be curious, because she'd be hidden and secret and mysterious. Then he'd stop by the stand and he'd say, Sophie? And she'd say, Yes? And he'd say, Sophie? How are you doing? Sophie!

And she'd smile and say nothing.

Fourteen

Don Porter, the old bird who lived downstairs, stopped Willis in the hall to complain about Zola. He had thin, slicked-back hair and a big, battered nose. "Your dog is walking on my head. You're not supposed to have dogs in this house."

Willis didn't know about that. He just looked at Don.

"Well?" Don said.

"Well, what?"

"What are you going to do about it?"

Willis pushed past him. If Zola was making Don crazy, he supposed he'd have to move, but he wasn't telling Don that.

It had been rainy and damp all week, and he hadn't taken Zola out much. Maybe that was the trouble. Zola needed her exercise, too. She could stand now. One back leg was still weak. He took her out on the new leash and gave her a walk on her three good legs. Then they sat on the steps. Zola kept turning and sniffing the air like it felt great to be alive.

He was teaching her to shake hands when Jim, his landlord, drove up. Willis got tense right away. Jim didn't come here that often. Don must have complained about Zola. "Give him a nice smile, Zola," Willis whispered, as Jim got out of his truck.

Jim came up the stairs with a lock and some tools. He was a chunky guy in a plaid shirt and green work pants. Willis hadn't exchanged a dozen words with him since he'd moved in. "Your dog?" Jim asked.

Zola backed under Willis's legs.

"I don't allow no dogs around here. Dogs can dig up a yard faster than a skunk."

What yard? On one side of the house there was Jim's trailer and on the other side an empty, weedy lot with an old car sitting in it. "She's not digging up the yard. I don't let her out by herself."

"Dogs can wreck a place faster than a kid."

"You want me to move? I'll move."

"Who said anything about moving? I was talking about dogs in general. I like dogs. What kind of dog is it?"

Willis stroked Zola's sharp little ears. "Sort of a purebred."

"Purebred! That'll be the day. He's a mutt. Craps all over, doesn't he?"

"She," Willis said. "No, she doesn't."

"You telling me he doesn't crap?"

"Her name's Zola. Shake hands, Zola." Zola put out her paw. "She's smart," Willis said. "I just taught her that."

Jim started installing a new lock on the door. "You

think it's easy being a landlord? People complain all the time. How am I going to satisfy everyone?" He squatted down and removed the old lock. "Today, it's the dog. Yesterday, it was the door. Tomorrow, it'll be the lot. Why do I let the weeds grow? What am I going to do about that car? Do you know how many complaints I've had on that car alone? How am I going to sell the lot with that wreck sitting there?"

"Why don't you call the junkman?"

"What, and give away a good car? All it needs is brakes."

"That's no big deal."

"And where am I going to get the time to fix it? Between this place and my job and my house, I'm going ten different ways."

He went back to the lock, and Willis sat there, uncertain where he and Zola stood. Were they going to have to move? Was Jim going to make an issue of it?

"You want that old car?" Jim said.

"Me? You selling it?" He didn't have any money for a car.

"I'll give it to anybody who'll get it out of the lot. I hate to just throw it away. It'd be good for a kid like you."

They talked about the car. Willis would have to fix the brakes, get the car inspected, find someplace else to park it.

Willis didn't say too much. He was thinking. He didn't know if he wanted a car. But that wasn't the point. It was a trade-off. His landlord hadn't come out and said it, but Willis knew it was either take the car, or you and your dog move out. By the time Jim had changed the locks, the car was Willis's.

Jim gave him the keys, and he and Zola went over to check it out. The car had originally been gold, but it had been sitting out in the weather so long it had faded down to a blotchy white. The rocker panels under the doors were chewed up and the tires were flat in back, but the rubber looked okay.

He unlocked the door. Zola sat in the passenger seat as if she knew all about rides. Willis turned on the ignition. Nothing. The car was dead. The gas gauge showed a quarter of a tank, but the engine wouldn't turn over. "Maybe there is no engine," he said to Zola.

He pried up the hood. The engine was all there, a big rusting lump. The battery probably had to be replaced. He hoped that was all there was wrong with it. He was having second thoughts, and third and fourth.

He brought Zola upstairs and went out running. It was raining again. That car was really a wreck. What do you expect—you got it for nothing. Yeah, but fixing it up was going to take a lot of time and money. Time he needed for running. Money he didn't have. And what was he going to do with a car? Every time he drove someplace, instead of walking or running, he'd be going backward, losing muscle tone.

When he came back from running, Sophie was standing in his doorway. She had a red scarf thrown across her shoulders. "Hi, Willis." She gave him a quick smile.

"Hi."

"Sophie," she said.

"I know. How did you figure out where I live?"

"I was on the block."

"You followed me."

"No . . . I just saw you." But she couldn't look him in the face.

He didn't really care. After he ran, nothing bothered him. Lots of endorphins, cheerful chemicals. He was heated up and loose and feeling good. She looked appealing, too, her face wet, water caught in her hair and lashes. She looked better than he remembered.

He opened the downstairs door, held it for a moment. "You want to come in?"

"Oh!" As if that hadn't been in her mind from the beginning. "I guess so." She shook out her scarf. "Just for a minute. I can meet Zola."

"I told her you might come." He couldn't resist a little teasing. He pulled off his sweatshirt and mopped his head with it.

As they were going up the stairs, snoopy bird Don came out to look. Came right out in the hall. "Is that you, Pierce?" he said, but he was looking at Sophie. "Well? What'd Jim say?"

"The dog stays." Willis couldn't help smiling. That moment alone made it worth taking Jim's car.

Don went into his apartment and slammed his door.

Fifteen

"I brought you a present," Sophie said.

"A present? What for?"

She brought out a plastic bag from under her jacket. "It's for helping me. Cookies. I hope they didn't get ruined by the rain."

"Can't you forget that? I don't want anything for what I did."

"You don't want the cookies? Feel them, they're still warm. They're old-fashioned gingerbread cookies."

He put the key in the lock. Zola was scratching on the other side of the door. "You made them?"

"Well . . . in a way. Is that your girlfriend I hear?"

That got a snort out of him. One for you, Sophie. The minute he opened the door, Zola came bursting out, barking and frisking around, so excited she fell down. "Hey, Zola, quiet down. We've got company. Give us five." The pup held out her paw.

Sophie squatted down, got her face right next to Zola's and kissed her.

"Careful," he warned. "I don't know how she is with strangers. I'm training her to be a guard dog."

Zola licked Sophie's hand, then rolled over on her back for Sophie to scratch her belly. "Some guard dog," Sophie said. She looked around. "Do you sleep right in this room? What's through that door? Your kitchen?" She sniffed McDonald's hamburgers and went to look out the window. She noticed everything. She noticed the lot next door and the car. So he told her it was his and how he got it. "I'm going to get it running again."

"I could help you fix it up," she said.

"What are you, a mechanic?"

"I like to do things. I've been around machines all my life. You know, you could have a garden out there. Where I live, there's no place for a garden. This is much nicer. I like it here."

"Hey, you shouldn't talk like that. You come here, you bring me cookies, you come right into my apartment. You don't even know me."

"That's what you said last time. And do you remember what I said last time?" She held out the bag of cookies. "Just sniff them. And then tell me you don't want any."

"I stay away from sweets. If you wanted to bring me something, you should have brought me a pizza."

"You've got enough pizzas." She opened the freezer compartment. "Look at that! All you've got here is pizzas."

He took a cookie and sniffed it. "It smells homemade. Is this a recipe you got from your mother?"

She shook her head.

"They sure smell good."

"I know."

"My mother used to make cookies sometimes," he said. "Sugar cookies. Vanilla sugar cookies. What do you call these?"

"Old-fashioned gingerbread cookies. Willis, I'd better tell you. I didn't make them. I bought them at Buttercup Bakery."

"Wait a minute! You said you baked them."

"No, I didn't. I didn't say it. I'm not that good a cookie baker."

"I thought you farm girls all knew how to bake cookies."

"I don't know about that. I don't like to bake that much." She sat on the windowsill. "What I like to do is fly."

"Fly?" he said. "Like an airplane or a bird?" And he flapped his arms. "What do you do, get up on the barn roof and flap your wings? *Cock-a-doodle-dooo*," he crowed.

She crossed her arms. "I didn't make fun of your running!"

"Oh, sorry," he said, but he couldn't stop it. Sophie flying? He saw her flapping over a barn or perched in a tree. Did she do it in the morning when the sun came up? He couldn't help himself. He did it again, flapped his wings and made like a rooster.

She sat there giving him a long, frowning, disappointed look. "What's so funny, Willis? You love to run. I love to fly."

It broke him up all over again. He went around the room like a jerk, flapping his wings. He was so bad she finally started to laugh, too.

"Some bird," she said. "You'd never make it off the ground."

He collapsed on the floor. "So tell me about this flying," he said.

"Do you really want to hear? I took some flying lessons. And I loved it. I'm going to be a pilot someday."

"You fly airplanes." He looked at her, kept looking at her, kept trying to put her in the cockpit of an airplane. "What kind of planes do you fly?"

"A Cessna 172."

"Why?"

"Why what?" She was getting mad again. "Why do I fly? Why do you run?"

"No, I mean, are you going to be something? A crop duster?"

"Are you going to be a messenger boy, Willis?"

Willis didn't know what to say. "That's great," he finally said. "It is. I was a little surprised. I mean . . . you know . . . but that's great. Why shouldn't you fly?"

"Oh, thank you, sir."

He was scrambling for position. Their relationship had suddenly changed. He was supposed to be the big knowledgeable city cat, and she was supposed to be the dumb little country mouse. He slid down on the floor and propped himself up on an elbow. "Flying! That's great."

"Someday maybe I'll get my license."

"Sure you will."

"I don't know. I've got to solo first, and you have to do a lot of solo hours—even go cross-country for about three hundred miles."

"That much?"

"At sixty dollars an hour it's going to take me forever to save up enough money." She looked up at the poster of Aaron Hill. "Who's that?"

"A great runner. He's a champion." He told her about

Aaron Hill and then about how he tried to match everything Aaron Hill did. He was telling her something he'd never told anyone else. Was he trying to make up to her for laughing at her? "Aaron Hill's my hero," he said.

"Does it get boring sometimes, running so much?"

"Do you get bored flying?"

She shook her head and stroked Zola's ears. A little silence fell between them. She looked out the window. "Well," she said, "I ought to go." She got up and arranged the cookies on a plate and then handed him one.

He took a bite, then gave Zola a bite. "What do you think, Zola?" Zola looked up for more.

"Zola likes the cookies," Sophie said.

"I do, too."

"You mean it?"

Under her jacket, she wore a flowered blouse open at the neck. Her neck was smooth and soft and invited his eyes to look.

"You like them?" she said.

He kept looking at her. He liked looking at her. He kept getting these little jolts in his stomach. "Listen," he said, "thanks for the cookies."

A few minutes later, she left.

He stood at the window and caught a glimpse of her on the other side of McDonald's. She bounced as she walked and swung her arms like she owned the street. Nice. He stuck his head out the window and yelled. "Sophie. Hey, Sophie, look up here." But a truck got in the way, and when it was past, she was gone.

Sixteen

"Doing anything this weekend?" Benny asked as they left work Friday afternoon. "Got something exciting on for the weekend?"

"I'm going to work on my car." Nothing had been said about the night the four of them had gone out.

"Come on, man. Dore saw you at the market, shopping with a girl. So, what's her name?"

"Who?"

"The girl you were with in the market."

"Oh, her."

"Who is she?"

Good question. Who was Sophie, anyway? A girl who worked in a newsstand, someone from the country who had stepped into his life. Or flown. Sophie, the flying bird. "Her name is Sophie," he said.

"Sophie, that's nice. Good-looking?"

"Not bad." He thought of her, poking around in his

apartment, looking into everything with that bright, loud way of hers.

"So, how tight are you two? Is that why you and Dore didn't hit it off?"

"Could be." He remembered Dore and her pink fingernails, and then he thought of Sophie again, and of how easy she was to talk to, easy to be around. Even when she got mad about the flying thing, it blew over fast.

Benny studied Willis. "You seeing a lot of her?"

"She was up at the apartment the other day."

"Your apartment?" Benny looked at Willis like that was the ultimate.

"She brought me a bag of cookies."

"Oh, sure, cookies." Benny tapped Willis on the shoulder. "You're a close number."

At home that night, Willis threw a frozen pizza into the oven and flipped on the TV. When the pizza was hot, he grabbed a can of soda and sat on the floor. Zola came sniffing around, and he gave her a bite of the pizza.

He heard somebody on the stairs. What if it was Sophie? He got up and put on a shirt. He checked himself in the mirror and went to the door. The landing was empty.

He shut off the TV and fell facedown on the mattress. He was disappointed. It was true. He wished Sophie was here. Sophie? He thought of all the girls he'd looked at and never spoken to. What did you say, anyway? Go up to a girl and say, You're cute, you want to come home with me? There were guys who did that, but he never could. It was too crude, too obvious.

Then he thought of the way Sophie had come to him. No invitation. He didn't have to do anything. She just walked in.

Yes, he said to himself, you had her right here and you let her get away.

He hadn't been nice enough to her. She had had to beg him to take the cookies, and then he'd laughed when she told him she was a flier. What a fool he was. She was probably never going to come back.

The thing was, after she left, the apartment felt really empty. It had always been empty, but now the emptiness bothered him. He went to the window and looked out, imagining that she was out there on the street. The feeling got so strong that he went downstairs and took a walk around the block, looking for her.

In the morning, he and Zola went out. She was maneuvering around on three legs. Every couple of steps, she stopped to sniff or scratch herself or lick her bad leg. The idea was to give Zola some exercise, get strength back in her legs, but she dawdled so much he finally scooped her up. "Doesn't it make you ashamed, being carried, a big girl like you?" She licked his face. "You horse."

In the park, Zola went crazy. She dove into the grass, then headed straight for the pond, where a girl with a red scarf over her shoulders was feeding the ducks. It was Sophie. When she saw Zola, she turned and looked for Willis, then waved. He waved back. It was like magic. He'd been thinking about her and here she was.

He wanted to go down to her, but he held himself back and started running, instead. He didn't want her to think he was that eager. He hated looking foolish. It was a mile around the pond. When he had circled five times, he went down to her. She was sitting on the grass. "Hello, Sophie."

"Willis." She shielded her eyes from the sun. "You ran a long time."

"Just five miles."

"Just! I can't do that."

"You could if you worked at it."

She laughed a little. "We seem to go to all the same places. I just discovered this park."

"I run here all the time," he said.

Nearby, a couple of skinheads in studded denim jackets were throwing stones into the water and looking over their way. "Those guys bothering you?" he said. "They keep looking over here."

"They like Zola. They wanted to know what happened to her leg."

"What business is it of theirs? You shouldn't have said anything to them. I wouldn't give those two the time of day."

Sophie reknotted her scarf. "You know, you keep telling me things. Just like my brother, Floyd."

"Is that good or bad?"

"It's a waste of breath."

He felt as if she was laughing at him. "Zola," he yelled. The dog was in the water, barking at the ducks. "Come on!" Zola looked around and went back to playing. He clapped his hands together. If the dog had any consideration, she'd come just to make him look good. "Zola!"

"She's still a puppy," Sophie said.

"She has to learn to follow commands. Zola! Come!"

"We never trained our dogs, and they never gave us any trouble."

"This is the city. You don't talk to strangers and you don't let your dogs run wild."

She got red in the face. "You're telling me things again."

"Forget it," he said. "I'm not telling you anything. Come on, Zola!" He'd come bouncing down from the path and now he felt like he'd landed flat on his face. She was mad and he was mad. Then Zola came running back and started shaking water all over them.

"No," Sophie said, and at the same moment they both reached down to quiet Zola. "She's such a nice dog," Sophie said.

"Well brought up," he said. "Not like her owner."

"Oh, her owner isn't that bad."

Willis twirled his cap on his finger, then, impulsively, he put it on Sophie's head.

"Oh, is that for me?" She fooled with it. "How does it look?"

"Good, but I'm not giving it to you."

She set it firmly on her head. "I like it. Maybe I'll get one myself."

"You can't. I've never seen another one."

"Where'd you get it, then?"

"The guy I bought my Raleigh bike from gave it to me."

Sophie stood up and looked at the sky. "It's going to rain."

Willis squinted disbelievingly. There was just a fringe of clouds in the west. "If it rains, I'll eat my cap."

She rolled her eyes and gave him the sort of smile that made him think she was just a kid. "How old are you?" he said to her.

"How old do you think I am?"

"Saying that means you're older than I think. I think sixteen, so it must be seventeen."

"Guess again."

"Well, you can't be fifteen, so it must be eighteen."

"Guess again."

"Nineteen? You don't look nineteen."

"How does nineteen look?"

"Look at me," he said. He was eighteen, but he wanted to keep things equal.

"You're nineteen?" she said.

"How old do you think I am?"

"I thought you were older. I'm older."

"How much older?"

"Older."

He took a wild guess. "Twenty-two?"

She nodded.

That was old—and interesting. A lot more interesting than sixteen.

A breeze rippled toward them, across the pond. "The sun's still shining," he said, but the sky was clouding over. Then there was a spatter of raindrops across the pond. "It's not going to rain," he said.

She handed him back his cap. "How're you going to eat it? With ketchup or mustard?"

The sky got dark and the wind started to blow hard, bending the trees. And then there was lightning and a slow, distant rumble of thunder. Willis scooped up Zola and they ran for the park shelter.

A boy and girl were sitting on a table inside. The boy's mouth was red and the girl had her hand under his shirt. They were just a couple of kids, about thirteen or fourteen years old.

Willis pulled his jacket off and dried Zola. Sophie walked around shaking out her hair. It was raining hard now. The windows were blurred with water. "Don't tell me it's raining," he said.

"It's raining," she said.

"Okay, you can be the weather expert," he said. "I'll give you that. You can have cows and horses and all that farm stuff, too."

"Also planes," she said.

"I get running," he said.

"And you get the city. That's your department."

From the corner of his eye, he was watching the kids. Now they had their arms around each other.

"What else do I have wrong about you?" he said. "You're twenty-two and you're a flying farmer. So you didn't have to ask your parents about coming to the city."

"I couldn't ask them. My parents are both dead."

"Oh, sorry about that. You're an orphan."

"I don't think of myself that way. What about your parents?" she said quickly.

"They're in North Carolina."

They sat in silence. Then he reached over and kissed Sophie on the neck.

"You know what?" she said. "I was just hoping you'd do that." And her face got red.

When the rain let up, they walked back to her house. She lived in an old building next to a parking lot. "Do you want to see my place? I'll invite you to supper. Oh, no, no, not tonight. I've got to clean up. How about tomorrow?"

"Tomorrow?"

She nodded. "Come around six o'clock."

In the middle of the night, he woke up, sure Sophie was in the bed beside him. Half awake, he felt her breath on his neck, and then he fell asleep again.

Seventeen

Sophie Browne is upside down . . . gone silly over Willy. Poor goose, she asked him to come to dinner and now she's in a tizzy. Fuss or no fuss? Do something? Do nothing? An elaborate meal? Simple meal? Prepare it now? Wait till he comes?

She had wakened early and couldn't go back to sleep. Her heart thumped; it shook her awake. He was coming. She was too excited to sleep. Willis was coming here today. Maybe. He was coming today. Certainly.

Or was he? She wanted him to come. Would he? Will he? Will he come? Willy, come!

Maybe he'd come. Maybe he wouldn't. She'd been too eager. She hadn't given him a chance to say anything. Yes, no, I don't know. . . . I'll let you know.

She knew. It was no. No Willy. No go. Poor goose! *Boo-hoo!* Nobody's coming to your party.

"Poor little worried duck," her mother used to say. Sophie remembered how she would make her mother laugh, waddling around the room like a duck, darting forward and quacking, looking out of the side of her head. Little bright duck eyes, her mother called her.

Rain spattered the windows. The king of Spain stays home in the rain.

Yes, he is coming, her mother said. He kissed you.

Maybe he was just feeling sorry for me. He's not coming—why should I do anything? Even if he comes, he'll probably stay five minutes, then run.

Now, Sophie . . . be calm. Set the table, why don't you?

Suddenly she longed for her mother, to be in her mother's house right now, to see her mother again on a Sunday morning, making dinner.

Bring another chair, Sophie, her mother would say. They'd make room for Willis at the table. Get Willis a cup, honey. Her mother never moved when Sophie was around. The mason jar of sugar would be on the table next to the economy-size jar of instant coffee. Willis would talk to her father and her brother, and she could sit there and watch him, and when he looked at her, she'd smile and ask him if he wanted another piece of white cake.

She went to the window, looked down at the wet parking lot. A car splashed through the puddles. When Willis had said, You're an orphan, she had wanted to put her arms around him and her head on his shoulder. It was true, she was an orphan. She missed her mother. She needed her mother. Now. Today. Mom, I'm entertaining a man. She had never entertained a man before. No, not entertained. Don't say entertained. It was an awful word. Like detained. Detrained. Derailed.

She was off the track again. She wasn't going to entertain Willis. That was too stuffy, too heavy, too scary. It sounded like a burial, like she'd invited him to a funeral.

Her funeral. She imagined herself greeting him dead. One of the walking dead, wearing a Dolly Parton wig, with a speaker in her chest. "How do? Why don't you-all come on in?"

All day she was like that, back and forth, like a water pump, back and forth, back and forth. She felt good. She felt glad. No, bad. Worse than bad. Scared. So scared she couldn't do anything.

When she finally stirred, it was to attack her head. That head! That hair! Like straw. Like something you stuffed in a mattress or put around tractor parts in a box. She hated the way her hair sprang out around her head. She had cut out an article in a magazine. Before and After, with pictures that proved it. Picture one—Before, ordinary. Picture two—they wrap a towel around her neck and shampoo her hair. Next picture, they cut. Snip a little here, snip a little there. Then the comb-out. Then the makeup. Then the miracle. Picture number seven—After. Ordinary woman is now striking, stunning, beautiful. Smiling, always smiling. A face that belonged on a magazine cover.

Sophie looked at the first picture again: ordinary. That was her. Then she looked at the next picture. Snip a little here, snip a little there.

She got the scissors and went to work. Snip, snip, here. Snip, snip, there. Then the makeup Pat had given her ages ago, before she even married Floyd. A little blusher, a little eyeliner. She worked cautiously at first, and then got bolder.

She stepped back to look at the results. What had she done to herself? She ran to the bathroom and washed her face. That part was easy. Her hair was hopeless. She put on a kerchief and tied it at the back of her neck.

And then it was time. There was no time left. She went to the refrigerator, made some hasty decisions. A spinach pie? Would he like that? But she should have cheese. No time to go to the store. Brenda. She ran down the stairs. "I'll return it tomorrow," she promised.

"What'd you do to your hair?" Brenda pulled the scarf aside. "You cut it. Hey, cute."

"Cute? It's awful."

"No, it isn't. I like it. Martin, look at Sophie. Doesn't she look cute?"

In her apartment, she made the pie, then mixed up a quick corn bread. If he didn't show up, she'd take it down to Brenda and the kids. Nothing gone to waste. Her eye scanned the kitchen. It was just a work space, an ordinary room, her plants crowding the windowsill. He'd never even notice. He wouldn't notice anything, because he wasn't coming.

Still, she washed the floor and put everything away. The table was in the living room. She'd bought it in a second-hand store; it had an enameled top and green legs. She'd found her easy chair right on the street. Somebody had thrown away a perfectly good chair. Ditto on the carpeting, a beautiful pink-rose color. She put straw mats on the table.

The last thing she did was get dressed. She put on a flouncy orange skirt and her strawberry blouse. Was Brenda right? She took off the scarf, then put it on again, then took it off. She didn't look at herself in the mirror.

She started watching out the window for Willis. When she saw him hopping across the puddles in the parking lot, she got scared. He was here! He and Zola. She ran to do ten things at once—a flame under the kettle, the fries on a pan to crisp. Oh, that spider plant was in the wrong place. She had it in her hand when she opened the door.

"Hello! Come on in! Oh, Zola, you're here, too! Where am I going to put this plant? You decide, Willis." Then she smelled the fries burning.

Eighteen

"Nice place." Willis spun around on his heel. Books and magazines on a table, plants, curtains, bright cloths, light and green things and good smells. By comparison, on a scale of Bad to Awful, his apartment fell off the charts. "Very nice, very nice." Ill at ease, he put on an air of slight superiority. The Inspector General, in sweats and sneakers, paced the room. He was still holding the plant. "Where do you want this?" But she was back in the kitchen.

"You really like my place?" she called.

"I do." He put the plant down on the floor under the window. "One thing for sure, Zola, she can use a few more plants."

"What about my plants?" Sophie said, coming back. "Do you want something to drink? I probably don't have it, but ask me, anyway."

"Water," he said.

"Water! Oh, that's easy. You can have all of that you want." She brought him a glass of water, then ran back for a glass for herself. "Now that you're here, should we have a toast?" She looked worried. "I don't know if that's right or not. Do you toast with water?"

"What's better than water?" He raised his glass and touched hers. "Let's toast Zola. Good health and long life to Zola."

She put down her glass. "Do you want the window open?"

She didn't hold still for a moment. Was it too hot in here? She fanned her face. What about the light? Enough light? She turned a light on.

"This room's about twelve by ten," he said. "I paced it out. Just about the size of mine."

"Too bad we can't put them together, we'd have one big room," she said, and the tips of her ears got red.

Nice ears, he thought. Then he noticed her hair. "You cut your hair."

Her hands went up. "Is it awful? Do you hate it?"

"No. Why do you say that? It's different."

"That means you don't like it."

"No, it just means I'm not used to it. I haven't seen it before. Give me a minute." He shut his eyes, opened them. "Hey, man! You cut your hair. Looks great!"

"He's teasing me, isn't he, Zola? Does he tease you, too?"

"Tell her I'm always teasing and I'm always serious."

"So, do you really like it, Willis?"

He got up and walked around her and took a good look. The Inspector again. Her hair was short and uneven, a little shaggy. He touched her head. "There are just a few uneven strands in back. Get someone to trim that for you."

"Brenda will," she said. "My friend from downstairs."

"I like it. It gives you a kind of free look. A city-girl look." Then, despite himself, he thought of Lee. City girl.

The photo of a guy in uniform with his head shaved caught his eye. Boyfriend? Former boyfriend? He didn't like the face. "Who's this dude?"

She took the picture. "Floyd."

"Oh. Your brother. I like his haircut."

"Do you?"

"Not really."

Another little silence fell. It looked like she was going to run again. "Let's sit down," he said.

"Do you like your job, Willis?"

"It's okay. Do you like yours?"

"Oh, yes!" She jumped up and moved the plant he had put on the floor. "How do you like living alone?"

"It's okay. How about you?"

"Oh, no! I miss people. Well . . . I do like having my own place. You're not really alone, are you? You have Zola. She's company."

"What kind of company is a dog?" He looked down at Zola, who was curled up at his feet. Good thing she didn't understand English.

"I should get a dog. I always had a dog. Did I tell you that before? Tell me if I'm repeating myself."

"I never lived on a farm," he said. "What do you do on a farm?"

"You're never bored."

"Same thing in the city," he said. "It's exciting. Step out of your apartment and you can get mugged, run over, or choked to death by the smog." He checked her out. She was laughing. He still liked making her laugh. "Yeah, my favorite smell is bus fumes, followed by fresh gasoline."

She flew out again to check the oven.

"Smells good," he called.

"As good as bus fumes?" She returned with orange slices on a plate.

The meal was good. She'd made spinach pie—he never thought he'd like that, but he dug right in. And there was hot corn bread with lots of butter. "Great meal," he said.

There was a knock on the door. "Yoohoo," someone called. It was Sophie's friend Brenda, a small, pale woman in jeans and a plaid shirt. "How're you doing? I came up to see if you need anything."

Willis pushed back his chair and stood up.

"Sit down, sit down, Willis," Brenda said, as if she'd known him forever. "Willis, you like this place? You wouldn't believe what a dump it was when this girl moved in. Sophie's really turned it into a palace."

"You want to have dessert with us?" Sophie said.

"Is it the tutti-frutti I gave you? No, thanks. I've had it up to here with that ice cream. Why do you think I gave it to you? I just wanted to meet Willis."

"Well, here he is." Sophie's ears were red again. Willis got a little hot around the collar, too.

When they were cleaning up later, Sophie started to sing, "Ta-ra-ra-boom-dee-ay. We have no school today. Our teacher passed away. She died of tooth decay. We threw her in the bay. She scared the fish away. She's never coming out. She smells like sauer . . . kraut!"

"Come on, sing with me," she said.

On the last stanza, he was yelling and Sophie was laughing, and he threw his soapy arms around her and hugged her. Maybe he could have kissed her—he should have kissed her—but he let the moment pass.

When he left, she went downstairs with him. "Is your car here?"

"Still working on it." He paused at the foot of the stairs. "I had a good time," he said. "It was really nice."

"You don't think I poisoned you?" She was a step above him, her hand on his shoulder. Her arm went around his neck and she kissed him.

Nineteen

The gate at the college track was chained, and Willis jumped the fence. The sky had begun to clear. The moon went in and out of the clouds. He was eager, aching to run at top speed, but he held himself back, setting a regular pace, slow at first, feeling better and better as he circled the track.

It was good to run . . . good to run . . . good to run. Good to stretch out, to break free. Thoughts flitted through his mind. Sophie . . . Sophie's kiss. He could still feel her arm around his neck. No girl had ever kissed him like that, held him and kissed him. He felt the glitter of tiny chemical explosions in his stomach. It was good to run and to remember the kiss, and run and feel the track under his feet, and run and feel the damp air chill against his cheeks.

He circled the track several times, his motions smoother at each turn, the beats of his footsteps and his heart indistinguishable. And then, behind him, like an echo, he heard another beat, the faint but steady slap of another runner's feet. When Willis was on the straightaway, he was on the turn. When Willis was on the turn, he was on the straightaway. He stayed behind Willis, not falling back, not coming ahead, either, letting Willis set the pace.

Was it a race? The moon disappeared in the clouds. Willis ran steadily. He didn't look back. Who was it? He knew and was afraid to look. *Aaron Hill.* Who else ran at midnight?

The back of Willis's neck turned to ice. Aaron Hill. Had the word gone out? Had Aaron Hill heard about the Midnight Miler? Was he checking him out? Checking out the competition? The Midnight Miler had announced himself, and now Aaron Hill was here to see what he could do.

As they passed the stands, the moon came out from behind the clouds. The track and the stands were illuminated. A light full of shadows filled the stands with silent, cheering fans. Fans everywhere, on the edge of the field and on the hillside and in the shadows of the houses.

And then Aaron Hill was moving up on Willis. He was roused, he was going to crush the challenger. Willis heard him coming. The slap of Aaron Hill's footsteps, his breath like a hammer in Willis's ears. He was gaining, gaining, gaining. Willis felt the air trembling behind him.

He turned. Looked.

There was nobody. The track was empty. He was alone.

Then, beyond the finish line, he caught a glimpse of something moving. A shadow. Something black, glittering in the fading moonlight, disappearing past the fence.

Twenty

Sophie liked the way Willis looked in his gray sweats and the white Raleigh bike cap. They were in the diner across the street from the stand, and he had Zola in his arms. "My treat," Willis had said when he stopped at the newsstand.

She wished he'd given her more notice. She had just finished work, and she was wearing her green cords and a baggy black sweater with the sleeves pushed up.

"I'm not very hungry," she said now. "I'll just have a soda."

"No, no, no. I want you to eat something, a real meal. Like the meal you made me."

They looked up at the menu board. "Zola recommends the open beef sandwich with gravy and mashed potatoes," Willis said. "No, wait," He bent to listen to Zola. "She's just changed her mind. She wants you to have the knockwurst with sauerkraut. And a nice gooey dessert, too."

Right on cue, Zola put a paw on Sophie's arm and looked appealingly at her.

"You taught her that, didn't you?" Sophie said.

"Sophie! Don't you think she's got a mind of her own?"

Sophie took big, warm Zola in her arms and sat her on a chair between them. Willis set a hot dog in front of Zola. She put her paws up on the table and sniffed.

"This is her first time eating out," Willis explained. "Her table manners aren't too good."

Willis ate fast, head down. Sophie liked the way he ate. When he ate, he ate, no nonsense. Sophie pushed the food around on her plate and fed Zola. She was too excited to eat. She and Willis were sitting close together, taking turns petting Zola. Sometimes their hands met, their fingers brushed against each other, but it was accidental.

Willis hadn't hugged her when he met her, caught her hand, or touched her. Nothing.

She kept wondering—was he glad to be here? Or was it just a duty? Payment in kind for the meal she had made? She'd noticed how careful he was about keeping things equal. The quarter he was so careful to pay back. And the cookies he didn't want to take. And now this meal.

He put his arm across the back of her chair, and she leaned back and thought about the kiss. Was he thinking about the same thing? "Did you run today?" she said.

"First thing this morning."

When their eyes met, he smiled. He looked sad till he smiled. He had a sweet smile.

"There you are, Sophie." It was Carl, her boss. He'd been at the stand, checking the week's receipts. "I thought you were in here." He took a chair from the next table and sat down and started talking business. "I'm increasing the morning paper order, so you double-check on Monday, make sure the count is right." He looked at Willis. "Who's your friend?"

She introduced them. "Willis, this is Carl, my boss."

They shook hands across Sophie. "Your girlfriend's a helluva good worker," Carl said. "Sales have gone up since she's been on the job. Hey, look at her blush. I didn't know girls still did that." He put his arm around her. "I could use ten Sophies."

Sophie was blushing. She got along well with Carl. He was like a big, plainspoken country man with a big belly and a big voice.

"Willis?" Carl said. "Willis Pierce? I used to know a Pierce. In real estate. Any relation?"

Willis shook his head.

"Where do you work? I'm always looking for good people. Young people. With me, maybe you start low, but I give you responsibility, you're on your own, and you can work yourself up.

"I've got a job," Willis said. "I work in Continental."

"What do you do there?"

"I'm in shipping."

"Shipping! What do you do, put labels on packages? Where's that going to get you? Where are you going to be ten years down the road? That's what you want to think about." Carl tapped himself on the head. "The brain. It's a wonderful tool. Use it."

Sophie watched Willis. Did he see what a character her boss was? There was a pained look on Willis's face. He was looking blankly at a Greek travel poster on the wall. Stone houses and mountains. She nudged Willis with her foot and smiled, telling him with her eyes, It's only Carl talking.

"George," Carl called. "Three beers."

"Not for me," Willis said.

"Free Lowenbrau? I'm buying. You don't turn down a good beer. Bring him one," he said to George. And then he said to Willis, "Once you try it, you're never going to drink that soda stuff, that baby sugar water, again."

Willis stiffened. Sophie saw it, saw the change in him. He didn't say anything, but she knew something was wrong. Then he looked at her. And what a look he gave her—as if he blamed her. For what?

The beer came. "Drink up, Sophie." Carl patted her shoulder. "You know what?" he said to Willis. "You don't smile enough. People who work for me smile. Look at that smile on Sophie."

Was she smiling? She didn't feel like smiling. What was wrong with Willis? It was like a gate had fallen between them. She leaned toward him. She wanted to put her arms around him and say, What's the matter? What happened? Why are you hurting? She wished Carl would leave so she could be with Willis.

But it was Willis who pushed back his chair, took Zola under his arm and walked out.

Twenty-One

Willis and Zola stopped a few doors down the street from the diner, outside Stankey's Bar. The late-afternoon shadow lay across the front. Willis was furious at Carl, furious at himself. Why had *he* walked out? Who had chased him? That bigmouthed boss of Sophie's had moved in on them, just sat down and taken over.

"I should have told him this was a private party." Zola looked up. "I should have told him, Sophie's not working now; she's on her own time."

Inside the plywood entry, the door to Stankey's was open. It was dark inside. The dark, malty smell of beer spilled out, and for a moment he was twelve again, watchful, angry, uncertain, waiting on the street for his father to come out.

He looked back for Sophie. Where was she? She should have come out with him. Instead, she just sat there and watched him go.

"Willis." It was her. He almost cried out, he was so glad to see her, and then he walked away.

"Willis!" She caught his arm. "Why'd you leave?"

He shook her off. "You had your boss. What'd you need me for?" He couldn't forgive himself for how glad he was to see her, and how ashamed and angry he was at himself for walking out instead of telling Carl off.

" 'Look at Sophie smile,' " he mimicked. " 'There's nothing nicer than young people smiling.' "

"I work for him," she said in a quiet voice. "That's the way he always is. It doesn't mean anything."

"You work for him! Does that mean he can paw you? He had his hands all over you."

She stepped back. "He did not."

"And you sat there like a frog and let him. Why'd you stay? Why didn't you leave when I did?"

"You just got up and left! I didn't know why you left."

"You didn't ask, either."

"You could have been going to the john."

"With Zola?"

"Okay! You could have been coming right back, for all I knew. I came out to find you. I only stayed there a minute with Carl."

"A minute too much."

"What's going on, Willis? Why did you call me a frog?"

"I didn't!"

"Willis. You just said it. I heard you."

"I don't mean half the things I say."

"Which half am I supposed to believe?"

"You figure it out."

"Willis. Willis." She was smiling. "Oh, I know what it is with you. You're jealous. You're jealous of Carl."

"Jealous?" he shot back at her. "Of what?"

It was like a slap in her face.

She stepped back, her hands up. She looked wounded. What had he done? What had he said?

Sophie was turning away, her eyes moving past him, and he was turning. In a moment, they'd walk away from each other, go their separate ways, and they'd never see each other again.

"Sophie . . . Sophie." It was all he could say. He didn't want to go on with this fight, and he didn't know how to stop it. "Sophie . . ." He held Zola out to her. "Sophie." He looked at her. "Sometimes I say things."

She stood there, half hidden, next to a telephone pole. He tried to take her hand. She moved away. He followed. They went around the pole. "Just now you looked at me as if you hated me," she said. She began crying, wiping her face and holding back the tears, and not letting him near her.

"No," he said. "No, I don't . . . I never . . ."

She sat down on the curb and blew her nose, and he sat down next to her with Zola between them. "I'm sorry," he said, and he tried to put his arm around her, but she wouldn't let him.

She got up. "I'm going home now."

"I'll walk with you."

"I don't care."

They walked along in silence. After a while, he said, "We were having a good time in the diner."

"Yes."

"Before he came, I mean. I was having a good time."

She nodded.

"How about you?"

"Me, too. Carl didn't have to come in."

"Well . . . We should have gone someplace else, where he couldn't find you."

"He could have waited for another time."

"Well, he wanted to talk to you. I shouldn't have been so jumpy."

She smiled a little smile. "You wouldn't drink his Lowenbrau."

They walked the rest of the way holding hands. They were like two tired swimmers who had just come out of a heavy sea. Their bodies ached, they were slow, their limbs were heavy and slow.

At her house, he wanted to go up with her. Did she want him to? "Well . . . good night," he said.

"Good night, Willis." She petted Zola. "Good night, Zola."

He turned away. He felt a heaviness descend on him. He could hardly move, but he kept walking. On the other side of the parking lot, he turned back.

"Soph?" He stood at the foot of the stairs, then started up.

"Willis?" She was there, waiting. Their hands caught and they held each other. Not talking. Just holding.

Twenty-Two

Unexpectedly, Willis's parents came to visit, arriving late Saturday with enough groceries to hold Willis for a month. They were on their way to Quebec to visit his father's family. "Why didn't you let me know you were coming?" Willis said. He put a box of cereal on the top shelf. "I've got to meet someone."

"You mean you're going to walk out on us?" his father said. "We just came."

Willis was shocked at how wasted his father looked. He'd always been spare, but now he looked skeletal, the tendons in his neck showed, and his jacket hung on him like it was sizes too big.

His mother kissed Willis. "Who do you have to meet? A girl?" While she unloaded the bag, her eyes took in the room. "Where's your furniture? This is it? It's nothing but an empty room. What do you need a dog for? Is he trained? I smelled dog as soon as I walked in. What's he doing?"

"She, Ma."

Zola was showing off, chewing on one of Willis's old sneakers. She brought it to Willis's mother and dropped it at her feet.

"Nice doggy," his mother said nervously.

"Zola's being friendly. She likes you, Ma."

His mother sat down. "Do you have some tea, Willis?"

He put the kettle on and showed her where the tea bags were, then rinsed a cup for her. "Ma, you want to make the tea? I've got to make a phone call."

He called Brenda from the Cleantown Laundromat. The dryers spun like pinwheels. A child answered the phone. "Who dis?"

"Get your mother. I want Brenda."

"Who dis?"

"Call your mother. Is this Jessie?"

"Who dis?"

He finally got Jessie off the line, and Brenda came on. "Oh, is that you, Willis? Sophie's right here."

"Hi," Sophie said. "I'm right here at Brenda's waiting for you. Where are you?"

"My parents just walked in. They're on their way to Canada and they're staying overnight with me. So I guess we won't go to that movie tonight."

Next to him, a man was folding underwear at a long table. Something about the man reminded him of his mother—the way his hands were busily doing while his eyes were miles away. That was his mother, always two steps ahead of herself, always anticipating the worst and girding herself for it. What would she say when she saw Sophie?

"Do your folks want to meet me?" Sophie said.

"They just walked in. I came right out to call you."

"Did you tell them about me?"

"I haven't had a chance."

"You're going to tell them, aren't you?"

"Sure I am." Why was she pushing? Why did he sound so defensive?

"Should I come over?"

"I don't know. They're tired. My father . . . they drove all day. They'll be leaving early tomorrow morning."

"You mean I won't see them? I won't meet your parents?"

"Did I say that?" He shifted the phone to his other ear. Everything he said came out wrong. "Look, Soph, I'll come over and get you. Now. In my car!"

On the way back, Sophie was too nervous to appreciate the car. "Willis? Do you think they're going to like me?"

"My parents? What do you mean?" Was he always this way? Asking a question when he was asked a question? He didn't know what his parents were going to think. He was wondering the same thing. Sophie was no dazzler. She wouldn't make anyone sit up and pay attention. When his parents met her, it would be like meeting somebody they had always known. Like meeting the neighbor across the hall who comes in to borrow a cup of sugar and ends up sitting down in front of the TV.

So what was wrong with that? Was he worried that they were going to judge her? Or him? Find her deficient and accuse him of settling for less than the best? Did they want to see him with someone like Lee?

"They're going to like you," he said. He blew his horn at the car ahead. "You haven't got reindeer antlers coming out of your head, Sophie."

"Do you think I'm dressed okay?"

"You don't have to fuss for my parents."

"Oh, I hope they like me."

Neither one of them should have worried. Willis's parents took to Sophie right away. She did exactly the right things. Gave his mother a big smile and said, "So you're Willis's mother!" And then she sat down with his father and started talking about welding.

"My dad taught me and my brother both to weld," she said. "If you live on a farm, Mr. Pierce, it comes in handy. Dad would never let me do the overhead stuff, though. He was always afraid I'd set my hair on fire."

"You weld?" Willis said. He'd never heard any of this.

His father laughed at him. "She's going to teach you, Willis, eh? We had one woman welding where I worked. She had been there since the war. A grandmother, and she welded."

"I remember her," his mother said. "They wrote about her in the newspaper."

His father started playing with Zola, and his mother went into the kitchen to cook supper. Sophie went in to help. "Willis, where's your dishes?" his mother asked. "This is all you've got? Two plates and one spoon?"

Sophie found some forks and four cups. Willis got a saucer from the bathroom. "Look, Ma, another dish." He didn't tell her it was Zola's.

The four of them ate together, sitting with their plates on their laps, Willis and Sophie on the floor and his parents on his mattress.

"Make believe we're camping out," his father said. "Like the old days." His father looked like a ghost, with his sunken cheeks, but his eyes still shone.

It was late when Willis came back from taking Sophie home, but his parents were waiting up for him. His father wanted to know what Willis was doing and who he was working with. He knew Miholic, the foreman. "Does he still run around like he's on roller skates? I knew him when he didn't know enough to tuck his shirt in. What did he promise you? Are you going to get upgraded? Are you bidding on jobs?"

"There aren't that many jobs right now. I'm lucky I'm working, Pop."

"I know, but still you bid on jobs, eh? Get experience. Get off that labor grade."

His parents were concerned about his future. What about those posters on the wall? Why didn't he have a chair to sit on? What about Sophie?

"You're going around in rags," his father said. "How can you go with a nice girl like that, the way you're dressed?" He stopped to catch his breath. "When you're young," he continued, "you think you have all the time in the world, but you don't, eh? The important thing is to have a trade and be with a good woman."

Later, changing the sheets on his mattress, his parents got really jolly. "At least we don't fall out of bed," his father said. He was a long time in the bathroom. Willis talked to his mother, who was in her nightgown. She was having another cup of tea.

"How is he, Ma?"

She shook her head. "The doctor says he's doing all right, but if you ask me, he had a bad winter. Everything hurt him. The least bit of cold and he's in misery. He's better now that it's warming up, but next winter . . ." Her downturned expression, the lines in her face, her hand ending the conversation—everything said there were things she didn't want to talk about.

That night Willis rolled up in a blanket by the window, Zola at his feet. His father coughed all night. In the morning, his father didn't want any breakfast. Not even a cup of coffee. He was nervous and anxious to go. "A whole day's driving ahead of us."

"Maybe you don't need coffee, but I do," Willis's mother said, and she poured a cup for him, too. The cup shook in his father's hand.

"We like your girlfriend," his mother said. "I hope we see her again another time."

"By then he'll have six more girls," his father said.

Willis watched his father go down the stairs, taking them one at a time, his shoulders bent. So slow. His father, who used to be so jaunty, the best-dressed man in the neighborhood.

"You stick with this girl," his mother said from the car. "Listen to your mother. You have somebody good there."

Twenty-Three

Sunday, with Willis directing her, Sophie drove the car out to the old, deserted Jackson Air Base on the flats north of the city. The roads into the base were blocked off by hills of dirt, but the motorcyclists and dirt bikers had chewed a path around them and that was how they drove in.

Inside the base, the roads were long and straight. A great place to run. Willis was excited by the road stretching out in front of him. He warmed up. Sophie was going to time him with the car, set a pace he would try to match. "Just push me. Don't let me get lazy."

He ran as fast and as hard as he could, keeping pace with the car. He was dripping when he finished, but exhilarated, and he wiped his head and his eyes and kissed Sophie. He felt totally relaxed, totally alive. He had Sophie and he had the running and he had everything.

"You're salty," she said, tasting his lips.

He lay back and let himself be kissed.

Later, when he left Sophie at her place, he noticed a pull in his right leg. By the time he got home, his whole leg was aching.

Dr. Waring asked Willis to cross his ankles and touch his toes. "Where do you feel the discomfort?"

Willis touched his right leg. "Here."

The doctor went straight to where it hurt, sending exquisite shooting pains down Willis's leg and back up into his buttocks. The doctor had the hands of a football player.

"How much running do you do?"

"Four to six miles Monday, Wednesday and Friday." That was stretching it a little.

"What else?"

"Eight to ten on the weekend."

"Saturday and Sunday both?"

"Yes." Everything he was saying was more or less true.

"What else?"

He hesitated. He didn't want the doctor to think he was some jerk who didn't know what he was doing, an office jock who only worked out on the weekend and ruined himself running. "I do some interval training."

"How have you been treating the pain?"

"I iced it when it first happened."

"And I suppose you went back to running?"

"Yes."

"You runners are all alike. If it hurts, make it hurt more."

Willis was silent. His leg was throbbing.

"Would you run if I told you that you had a fractured femur or that you'd cracked a bone in your foot?"

"Is that what happened?"

"No, I'm just trying to impress something on you. When

something hurts, stop. You've got an inflamed sciatic nerve."

That didn't sound too bad.

"I want you to stop running until the pain and soreness disappear."

"How long will that be?"

"I don't know. It may take a week. It may take two weeks. It may take two months. Depends on you."

"Two months! Because I've got a pain in the butt?"

"The more you rest, the faster you heal. Stay off your feet until that pain disappears."

"Stay off my feet! I have to work. And I can't run?"

"That's right. I know it's hard for you runners to get it through your skulls. You *cannot* run while that pain and soreness persist. That's what pain means. Your body is telling you something. Do you keep your hand in the fire when you feel the heat? The principle is the same here."

"Two months! What am I going to do for two months?"

"Swim," the doctor said.

Willis's Australian crawl was adequate; his head came up at every fourth stroke and his legs kept up a steady flutter, two beats to every arm stroke. He hated swimming laps. It was boring. There was nothing to see, no place to go. Round and round like a goldfish. Or was it a motorboat? Or an ape going up a tree, arm over arm?

He swam twice a day at the downtown YMCA, once in the morning before he went to work and again at night after family hour. He swam laps. That's what you did in a pool, up and back, then up and back again. What good could he say about swimming? Not much. Maybe he was staying in shape for running. Maybe he was sweating, but how could he tell?

The pool was old, the tiles were cracked and the locker room smelled stale and mildewed. Afterward, he smelled like he'd been dipped in chlorine. His eyes were always red. He bought a pair of goggles, and they helped a little.

He kept increasing the ante, putting the pressure on himself. Forty laps, fifty, sixty, a hundred. His head heated up and his arms beat the water like wooden paddles. He was having a workout, he was staying in shape, but he didn't believe it.

Sometimes Sophie came for family hour and they'd fool around in the pool together. Playtime, everyone in the pool, fathers and their little kids, old people keeping their arms and legs in motion, Willis and Sophie.

Tonight, she wore a yellow frilled cap and a black bathing suit. He couldn't get his eyes off her. He was supposed to be helping her improve her stroke. She did a sort of dog paddle with her head above the water. "Put your face in," he said, "the way I showed you yesterday. The dead man's float." He put his hand under her stomach to move her along.

"I can swim without putting my face in the water."

"No, you can't. You'll never be a good swimmer if you're afraid to swallow a little water." He demonstrated, showing her how to stretch out her arms and relax and let her head go under, then bring it up to breathe.

She tried, but she came up sputtering. "Forget it," she said. "You swim your way and I'll swim mine."

"I'll never understand it," he said. "You're afraid to put your face in the water, but you're not afraid to go up in an airplane."

"That's just the way I am."

"Let's try it again. The main thing," he said, putting his arm around her waist and letting his fingers spread over her hip, "the most important thing . . ." It was hard for him to think when he had his arms around her. "Is the breathing."

"The main thing," she repeated, smiling. "Always talking about the main thing." They kissed in the water, just their lips touched, and they kissed again. That was the end of swimming lessons for that day.

Twenty-Four

Every day now, Willis went out at lunch to be with Sophie. "Hey, Willis," Benny called after him as Willis punched out, "going out for lunch again? What's her name?"

"Who?" Willis said and kept going.

"Who—is that her name? Hey, Willis, don't run away."

Willis walked out to Spring Street and sat down on the stone steps opposite the newsstand. It was a cold day, windy, with a white scum over the sky. Sophie was busy, but gave him a little wave.

As soon as she was free, she came over and pulled him up, then sat down in his place.

"Hey, you took my seat."

"It's nice and warm. Want to sit in my lap?"

"No thanks."

"Sit down next to me, then. Down," she ordered.

"Arf. Arf."

She unwrapped one of the sandwiches she'd brought and divided it.

"Good," he said.

She leaned against him. "Is it on for tonight? You coming over?" She smoothed his hair and made a little braid in back. "You know what? Your right ear is bigger than your left ear."

"That's from hanging on the phone."

"Who are you calling? You don't call me."

"You don't have a phone."

"You don't either. Do you make all your phone calls from the Laundromat? Are there a lot of girls in there?"

"I never noticed."

"Liar." She pushed him. "You stand there with the phone to your ear and look at all the pretty girls. That's why you've got one fat ear."

"What about you?"

"What about me? I don't have fat ears." She pushed her hair behind her ears. "Are they fat?"

"They're nice. Did I tell you I'm going to start running again?" It had been only two weeks since he'd seen the doctor and his leg was already feeling better.

"I don't want you to start too soon," she said.

"I won't push it." He went over to the diner and brought back a couple of fruit tarts and a container of milk.

A few minutes later, Benny walked by, waved to Willis and gave Sophie a long look.

"Who's that?" Sophie asked. "He's cute."

Benny stopped. "Somebody calling me?"

Sophie's hand went to her face. "I didn't want him to hear that," she whispered to Willis.

Benny came over. "Is this your girlfriend, Willis?" He smiled at Sophie. She went into the newsstand and started arranging magazines. Benny peered in at her, and she put a magazine in front of her face.

"Sophie," Willis said, "this is Benny from work."

"Oh, Sophie," Benny said. "I remember now."

Was he teasing? Was he laughing at her? Willis didn't like it. "Hey, Benny," he said, "you've got someplace to go, don't you?"

"Not really."

"Yes, you do." He moved Benny along. "See you later."

"See you, Sophie," Benny called.

"Is he gone?" Sophie said, coming out. "Did you see the way he looked at me, Willis? He really looked me over."

"Oh, that's the way he is. You didn't have to hide from him."

"I was embarrassed."

"Guys like Benny, you ice them. That's the only way to be with them." Willis flipped the pages of a magazine.

"How would you know?" Sophie said. "You're not a girl."

Willis picked up a magazine, then dropped it. "I'm not from the country, either."

She gave him a look, then slapped a few magazines down on the counter.

He'd put his foot in it again. "So we're eating supper together tonight, right?" he said.

"Why? So you can give me some more advice?"

"Well, you have to admit you don't know how to hide anything. Why'd you act that way with Benny? You see guys every day. I've seen you with your customers. You don't have trouble talking to anybody. Why that big show for Benny?"

"It wasn't a show! I told you, he embarrassed me. My customers don't embarrass me."

"Well, you embarrassed me, too. He's going to give me the needle about that for a week."

"Oh, I'm really sorry for you," she said. "You want a candy bar?"

"What for?"

"To sweeten you up."

He laughed. "So, what time tonight?"

"I just remembered I'm going to baby-sit for Brenda."

"Since when?"

"Since just now."

"Good. Because I just remembered I couldn't make it, anyway. I'm going to get a haircut." He didn't have to look at her to know that they were in trouble. The whistle blew. "I'll see you," he said. Then, over his shoulder, "I might be back on time."

"For what?" she said, and she went back into the stand.

Twenty-Five

Haircut. He'd said it and now he had to go through with it. Right after work, he went to the old neighborhood, to the barbershop on Almond Street where he used to go as a boy to get his haircuts.

The barber snapped out the sheet and pinned it snugly around his neck. The fight with Sophie was gnawing at Willis.

"You want a trim?"

Willis looked at himself in the mirror. "Take it off."

"How much?"

"Skin it."

Later, when he could have been eating with Sophie, Willis was underneath the car fixing the brakes. If he got the car running soon enough, he'd go over to her place and make up with her. But by the time he was through messing around, it was too late.

Then, Saturday morning, he was on his way over to

Sophie's and the car started to smoke and then it died. He spent the rest of the morning just getting the stupid car off the street. He worked on it all afternoon. If anything else went wrong, he was going to run it off a cliff.

Later he cleaned up, and he and Zola drove over to Sophie's. She was outside, sitting on the steps with Brenda. She was wearing a green cardigan, the orange skirt and white sneakers.

Willis leaned over Zola and nodded to Brenda. "Hi. How're you doing?"

"You talking to me?" Brenda said.

"Anybody." He wanted to say something to Sophie, but she wasn't looking at him. "You haven't seen my new car before, have you?"

"Who?" Brenda said.

"You."

"New car? That heap?"

"It's new to me."

Brenda walked around the car and kicked the tires. "It's a car," she agreed.

"Well." He didn't get out. He didn't feel safe. "Zola really likes to ride in the car."

Sophie came over and petted Zola. "Hi, sweetie." She kissed Zola.

Willis gave Sophie a winning smile. "I was going to come over here yesterday."

"What for?"

He ignored that. "But I had to work on the brakes and I had trouble again this morning."

"You sure did," Brenda said.

"Well, I was just driving by. I guess you're busy."

"Mmm," Sophie said.

"What'd you have for supper Friday night?"

"What'd you have?"

"I forget. Pizza, probably."

"We had steak, french fries and strawberry shortcake. Fresh California strawberries and whipped cream."

"Sounds good."

"It was."

There was a short silence. "I was thinking about giving the car to you," he said.

"What?"

"Don't take it," Brenda said. "It sounds like a crooked deal."

"I don't need a car," he said to Sophie. "I run."

"You run everywhere?" Brenda said.

He wanted to strangle her. "I'm trying to get my legs back in shape, Sophie. You get too dependent on a car and you lose your running legs."

"You want Sophie to lose her running legs?" Brenda said.

"You want to come for a ride," he said to Sophie.

"Sophie hasn't got the time," Brenda said.

"How about you, Brenda? I'd like to take you for a ride."

"I'm a mother. I can't afford to risk my life."

Sophie was laughing. Having Brenda there was making everything impossible. "Brenda," Willis said, "you mind if I talk to Sophie?"

Brenda glanced at Sophie.

They must have been talking about him. What had they said about him? What had Sophie told Brenda? What had Brenda told Sophie? Willis gunned the engine and swung around the parking lot.

"What's that smoking out your rear end?" Brenda yelled.

He came back to Sophie. "Come on, Soph, we can't talk here. Let's go for a ride."

"Where?"

"Wherever you want."

After a moment, she got in and put Zola in her lap.

He drove out, wondering why it was so hard all the time. Were they always going to be fighting? Everything he said to her started a fight, and she didn't forget anything.

"I thought country girls were easygoing," he said.

"I thought city boys had brains."

Maybe there was something so wrong between them that nothing would ever make it right. That was such a lousy thought that he just pushed it away. He drove around a while longer. Neither of them said anything.

He parked by the concrete water tower up in the hilly part of town. He put an arm across the back of the seat and tried to kiss her.

She avoided him, bent down and fussed with Zola's collar. "You've got this on too tight. You'll choke her."

He reached down to loosen it.

"I can do that," she said.

He sat back, looking gloomily out the window. The water tower was covered with school graffiti. EAST HIGH GOES FOR IT! . . . BRAD, KEVIN AND ED, THE RAGING ONES . . . JULIE AND JERRY FOREVER.

"Should we put our names up there?" he said. "Sophie and Willis?"

"What for?"

"Tell the world."

"Who's going to believe it?"

He looked at her, then looked away.

Sophie held Zola in her lap.

"Zola, the lady over there," Willis said. "See if you can talk to her. See if you can make her like me."

Sophie bent down and whispered something in Zola's ear.

"What did she say to you, Zola? Was it something about me? How mean I am? She likes you, but she doesn't like me. Just because I'm not perfect."

That got a snort out of Sophie.

"Zola, tell her she's made plenty of mistakes herself. You, too, Zola. I don't get mad at you because you chew my sneakers. Maybe I yell at you a little, but that's all. Because I know how you are. You like to chew on things."

He reached over and scratched Zola behind the ears. Sophie was stroking her, too. In ecstasy, Zola rolled her eyes from one to the other.

Sophie said, "You love me, don't you?"

Willis said, "Who are you talking to, Zola or me?"

"I'm talking to Zola."

"Oh."

"But maybe you're included."

He got his arms around her and kissed her hard on the mouth.

She pushed him away. "No, don't."

"You don't want me to kiss you?"

"Not like that. And not when we're still fighting."

"Are we still fighting?"

"Well, we haven't made up, yet," she said.

"That's what I was trying to do when I kissed you." He could hardly remember the fight. He wondered if he should ask her what they had fought about. It seemed so insignificant now. So Benny came around and Sophie got embarrassed and he got worried. So what? "I'm a jerk," he said.

"No, you're not," she said quickly.

"Yes, I am. So Benny came around. I don't know why he bothered me. He can be a jerk, too."

"He sure acted that way."

"You won't believe this, Sophie. You should have seen the pictures he showed me of his girlfriend. In her underwear."

"No! Was it really his girlfriend?"

"He's not such a bad type, but he's sort of crude sometimes."

"Now we agree," she said. She leaned forward and kissed him. It was sweet. He pressed his lips against hers, and his cap fell off.

Sophie gasped. "Your head. What did you do to yourself?"

He felt his bald head. There was a bristle of new growth. "I fell asleep in the barber chair. Don't you like it?"

"The barber did it to you?"

He laced his fingers over the top of his head. "I told him to do it," he admitted.

"You told him! Why?"

"I don't know. Because you and I had a fight and I was feeling bad."

"What are you going to do next time we have a fight? Chop off your arm?"

"I'll think of something."

She stroked his bare head. "It looks cold," she said, "but it's warm and velvety, poor, little head." Then she kissed him on top of his head.

Twenty-Six

Up in Sophie's place, you get some definite ideas. You've had them before, in the pool and in the car, but never as strongly as now. The two of you are close friends now. You've eaten together . . . you've talked . . . you've kissed . . . you've done a lot of things together.

It's hard to get to know someone. You know it better than anyone, because you're not naturally friendly. What did that kid Rosenbloom say about you, years ago? That Willis Pierce was the meanest kid in Columbus Junior High? He wasn't kidding; he was telling the truth. That's you, you're not naturally nice. Not naturally loving. Not naturally anything. Everything you do, you do hard. But you want someone—oh, how you want someone.

You didn't love Sophie the second you saw her. You didn't know you were going to feel this way in the beginning. You didn't even like her. Then, after a while, you did, and you felt something. It's hard not to feel something when you're alone with a girl. It's hard not to feel something just thinking about girls. But you're thinking about Sophie now.

You know her now, and she knows you. And you've talked about your dreams and told her things you never told anyone. How you used to feel shorter than everyone, afraid you'd never grow, and how you were ashamed of your father and guilty. And she said, But you loved him, too.

And you agreed and you told her how you love to run and how good it makes you feel and how you dream about being famous, about doing something, just one thing, that people will know and remember about you forever.

And she's told you things about herself, too. How ignorant she feels because she never finished high school. And how she still misses her mother and how she was the only one in the family that got along with her father. And how much she misses flying, how when she was up there in the sky she felt as if the whole world belonged to her.

It hasn't always been perfect. You've gotten mad at each other plenty of times. Really, she's gotten mad at you more than you have at her, and why not? You've acted like a jerk, you've got a lot more to learn and you've said plenty of unfriendly things. But if she knew the times you wanted to say unfriendly things and didn't, she might not think you were so bad in that department.

The important thing was that you always came back. You made up with her. You kissed. You made her laugh. You held each other so tight it hurt.

Your place or mine, you think, even though you're at her place. *Your place or mine?* It's something you heard in a movie once. You liked it. It was so direct, so simple and straight.

Your place or mine, you think again, and you put your

arm around her. She's trying to pour milk into a dish for Zola, and the milk is spilling on the floor and Zola is licking it up.

You pull Sophie against you and you let your fingers spread around the roundness of her shoulder and down the back of her arm.

It isn't like you've just met. It isn't like you were grabbing from the first minute, with just one thing on your mind, even though it was there, in back of you mind, all the time. Now is the time, but you don't know how to talk about it and you don't need to talk about it. Your place or mine?

She puts her hand over yours circling low around her waist, presses it tight against her body. Then she releases herself and checks the refrigerator and cupboard. And she asks you if you're hungry.

But you're on the floor now, on your back, looking up at her hopefully. Your place or mine? You know that you're not good with words. In intimate matters, words get in the way. Words can be misunderstood. You haven't had that much practice, but in some things the body speaks a language of its own. A clearer language.

She lies down on the floor with you, and you lie there looking into each other's eyes. Her hand rests on your chest, and you've got one hand under her cheek. And you've never been happier, so you kiss her. But because you're eager and excited, your lips pop. You make her laugh, and she kisses you and pops her lips.

And you think *now . . . now . . . now.* And your heart is beating like a big drum. You're happy, and you think this moment is perfect and unlike any other moment that ever was or will be, and you say it and she nods in agreement and you feel how much you are in perfect harmony.

And just then the neighbors, the couple on the other side of the wall who, Sophie says, start fighting every Friday and keep it up until they go to church on Sunday, those neighbors start yelling and cursing and throwing things at each other. And you both have to listen because the walls are so thin it's like they're in the room with you. And they're saying things to each other that are not harmonious or loving. And there's pain on Sophie's face, and you're saying, How long is this going to go on? And she's saying, It could go on all night, and everything inside you shrivels and you say, My place.

And then at your place, you eat first because you're starved for everything now, but also because food is easier. You make pepper, steak and onion sandwiches on soft Italian rolls, and you sit opposite her, looking and chewing and catching her knees between yours. And you drink soda from one bottle and then you clean up together.

And by now the waiting is part of the doing, and her eyes are shining and her cheeks are soft and flushed and you turn out the lights and the street lights come in, and you kneel down together, facing each other.

And you're not thinking too good anymore; you're overheated the way you are after you've run hard and you feel the blood throbbing in your fingers and your lips.

And you think she's like you, because her lips are pressed hard against yours and she's murmuring something that's not words but like music, and you know that what you've been waiting for she's been waiting for, what you want she wants, and the feeling is like trying to talk about good music and not being able to get it right.

There are no words, no words that you know, there's only now, and that feeling that's shaking you like the rolling of the ocean, and you pull off your shirt, and your hands start doing things with her clothes. Only your hands are as dumb as you are, and you're too rough and too fast. Wait, she says, wanting to help, but you've pulled the arm of her blouse the wrong way and it tears. Her favorite blouse with the strawberries on it.

It doesn't matter, she says. And she lies against you, and all she wants to do is cuddle and get close, but her bare skin is like nothing you've ever known, and there are tears in your eyes, because it's more than you can contain, and you just hug her and hang on to her and say, Damn. And she says again it doesn't matter, and she says she's happy, and you can't talk because everything in you is spent and it's incredible, like the feeling you get some mornings when the sun is rising and the birds fly up as you run past.

Twenty-Seven

Every weekend Sophie and Willis drove out to the air base. It was their regular Sunday afternoon routine. He ran and she paced him with the car. Afterward, he changed and they went out to eat.

"My birthday's coming," Willis said, when they were in the restaurant.

"When? You didn't tell me."

"I'm telling you now. It's the twelfth."

"You're going to be twenty. No more teens. You're catching up to me."

"Not exactly." He looked at her over the top of the menu.

"What, Willy?"

"What what?"

"Not exactly what?"

"Uhhh . . . let's see what we're going to eat."

"You always order the same thing. You don't have to

look at that." She pulled the menu down. "What did you start to say?"

"My birthday's coming."

"You told me that already. And?"

"I'm going to be nineteen."

"No. You are nineteen."

"Ah . . . no. I lied. I'm eighteen. Going on nineteen."

"You lied to me?"

"Well . . . slight exaggeration. I wanted to impress you. I thought you wouldn't look at me if I was too young."

She reached over and pinched his cheek. "You're nothing but a baby."

Under the table, he bumped his knees against hers.

The waitress came over. "Double cheeseburger," Willis ordered.

"Avocado salad," Sophie said.

"Well," Willis said when the waitress left, "how fast did this baby run today?"

"I couldn't believe it. I had the car up to fifteen miles an hour and you were keeping up with me. Of course, you looked like you were dying."

"I was giving it everything."

"You should have stopped."

He mopped his forehead with a napkin. Water was still coming off him. "Pain is a part of being a really good athlete. Every game, every sport hurts, but that's not the point. You don't let it stop you. And when you get through it, there's no feeling like it. You feel great."

"You must love it when you have a toothache."

Their order came. He took a bite out of his sandwich, then inspected Sophie's salad. "Want some?" she asked.

"No, thanks. I wonder if the speedometer in the car is

accurate. I should buy a decent stopwatch. I keep getting different figures."

"Does it matter?"

"Not really." But a moment later, he said, "It would be nice to know how fast I'm really running."

"Very fast."

"That's the good thing about competition," he explained. "It makes you run harder and then you know how you stand."

"So why don't you go compete?"

"Why?" He looked at Sophie and slowly smiled. "Maybe I'm lazy."

Sophie burst out laughing at that idea.

"I've never done it."

"That's no reason. I never flew in an airplane, either."

"How's the flying fund coming along?"

She made a little face. "Oh, it's so hard to save money. I had to buy a toaster, and you know it was just Jessie's birthday. And Brenda's anniversary is coming up, and I want to get her something really nice. And now your birthday . . ."

"You don't have to get me anything. Birthdays don't mean anything to me."

"I noticed. You don't even know how old you are."

The waitress came with the check, but they sat there a little longer. "I have a feeling if I did race," he said, "I could take anyone. Any of those hotshot college boys."

"I bet you could," she said.

"If you want the truth, maybe even Aaron Hill." He laughed. "How's that for being crazy?"

"What's crazy about it?"

"Sophie!" He reached over and held her hand. "Aaron

Hill? We're talking world class. We're talking the best. We're talking Steve Cram and Sebastian Coe. We're talking about the greatest milers in the world."

"Maybe you're one of the greatest, and you don't even know it."

"Yeah, maybe I am." And he laughed again.

Twenty-Eight

Friday, on her way home, Sophie bought a snake plant, tall green-and-white blades. The plant reminded her of Willis. She liked the way it stuck up next to the other plants, head up and proud. Nothing cuddly there, nothing soft and easy. She put it near the rubber plant with its large, showy leaves. The rubber plant was Carl. "You two don't get along." She set the snake plant off by itself on a chair. "There, you're all by yourself, Willis, the way you like it."

Glancing out the window, she saw a familiar faded blue pickup truck in the parking lot. She recognized the truck first and then she saw her brother, looking around, hands in his back pockets, high-peaked John Deere cap set square on his head. She rapped hard on the window. "Floyd! Up here, Floyd."

She met him on the stairs, got her arms around him, sniffed hay and milk and motor oil.

He was stiff, that was the only way to describe it, but

she was too excited to care. She rubbed his back, smiling, pulled him upstairs. "You look great, Floyd. What have you been doing? How are things on the farm? How are Pat and the kids? Did she have the baby?"

He looked around her apartment. "Fancy place you've got here, Soph."

"Fancy!" She laughed. "You should have seen it when I got here. It took me the better part of a day just to carry out the garbage."

"Yeah? Where'd you get all the plants?"

"Bought them."

"Looks like you're going to open a store." He peered out the kitchen window. "Can't raise much corn in that parking lot." He shook the table. "Rickety thing, isn't it? Well," he said, looking at her for the first time, "how are you doing for yourself?"

"Fine," she said. "Good. I'm doing real good." And she waited. What was her brother doing here? It wasn't like Floyd to make this trip just to tell her she was eating off a wobbly table.

"You look like you lost some weight, Soph. Don't you eat?"

"All the time."

"And your hair? I never saw it that way."

Her hand went to her hair. "Do you want something to eat?"

"Oh, I think I could handle something."

She took out hamburger, cut some potatoes and onions, and put them on to fry.

"I don't get it," he said. "This place, the city—how can you stay down here? How do you even breathe the air?"

"I manage." She was the one who didn't get it. Floyd and Pat were the ones who'd wanted her out. Where'd they think she was going when she got on that bus? Down the road to the next farm?

"You wouldn't catch me down here," he said. "They'd have to nail both my feet to the ground to keep me in the city."

She put the food on the table, then started water for coffee. Floyd had barely looked at her place before he started knocking it. Then he let her know she wasn't one of the real people anymore because she lived here. Then he sat at the table and waited for his food to appear. She had always waited on him. She had just never thought about it before.

"You ever dry the dishes, Floyd?" She thought of Willis with a dishcloth in his hands.

He forked up potatoes. "Pat's getting close to her time. She doesn't come out to the barn at all anymore. I've just got John Towig helping me after school, and you know how much help he is. I've been coming in at midnight every night and I'm up at four to milk in the morning."

The complaints were familiar ones. That was home, that was the farm, more work than any two people could ever do. She sat down opposite him. With all his complaints, it was comfortable being with her brother.

"Where's the bread?" he said. "And the margarine?"

She jumped up again.

He folded a piece of bread around the hamburger, chewed, the muscles in his jaws dancing. "I don't know why you left. I told you I was going to fix up the garage for you. But you were so dead set on going."

"You needed the space." She hadn't forgotten the green ice she'd seen around Pat's face and the fire that seemed to leap out from under Floyd's collar when they'd all been together in the house.

"Well." He looked at his watch.

"Are you going? That's not much of a visit."

"I've got an hour, that's all. I've got to get back to do the milking."

"It was nice of you to come see me, Floyd. Maybe next time you'll bring the kids. Be sure to give Benjie and Alice big hugs from me."

"Pack up, Sophie," he said. "Come back with me and you can see them right now."

"What?"

"We need you there. You should hear Pat. Ten times a day she's calling you. 'Where's Sophie? I wish Sophie was here.' You don't have much junk, do you? How long till you'll be ready?"

Sophie went to the window. "Is that why you came?" She should have known. When had Floyd ever gone out of his way for her? When had her life ever meant anything to him? It was true, but it hurt. The only reason he'd come was to bring her back so she could work for them.

He didn't even ask if she would or she could, just took it for granted she would say yes. Yes. Yes, Floyd. Sure, I'll come back. Sure, I'll help out. The yes was on the tip of her tongue. All her life, she'd been saying yes to her family, yes to her father, yes to her mother (but that was different), yes to her brother. Yes, yes, yes.

The one time she didn't say yes, did what she wanted to do, was when her father was dead and Floyd was gone. Then she said yes to Sophie, took her money and started flying lessons.

"You didn't even ask me about my job," she said. "Aren't you the least bit curious?"

"Okay, what's this great job of yours?"

"Forget it. And I can't get ready that fast, either." Then

she thought, Willis. What was she going to tell him?

Her brother put down his cup. "You don't come now, you're going to have to take the bus then, because I'm not coming down twice. You have any jelly?"

She got the jar from the cupboard.

"What kind of jelly is this?"

"Pizza jelly." It was her joke with Willis. There was pizza jelly and pizza milk and pizza toothpaste.

"When'll you be home? Tomorrow?"

"No. Not tomorrow. I've got to tell my boss."

"Give him a couple of days. But no more, Soph."

She sat down. Pizza jelly, her job, her boss—he didn't care what she said. It was like he was in the barn, brushing the mosquitoes away. She didn't know what to do. She didn't want to go, but her brother needed her. "Can't you get anybody to help Pat?" she said.

"She wants you, Soph."

"What if I don't come home, Floyd?"

"What's the matter? Are you mad about something?" He got that little-boy look on his face. The what-did-I-do-wrong look.

"I'm here now. I'm not on the farm anymore. I'm going to come up for a few days when the baby comes. But I'm going to have to come back."

Floyd squinted at her, really looked at her, a cold look, pale around the eyes. All the warmth had gone out of his face. "So that's the way things are," he said. "I thought you'd be glad to come. Well . . . suit yourself." He put on his jacket and left.

Twenty-Nine

On the way over to the Winter Sports Dome, Willis showed Sophie a story he'd clipped out of the newspaper. Aaron Hill was coming back home in June to run in the Eastern College Regionals. "Look at him," Willis said. The picture showed Hill standing with his hands on his hips. "You see how relaxed he is, Soph? He's got the opposition all psyched out. Those other runners look at that picture and they know they're going to lose."

He could have quoted the article to her, word for word, he'd read it so many times. "I'm a runner," Hill had said. "I was born to be a runner and so I run."

Ever since Sophie had said that maybe Willis was a great runner and didn't even know it, he'd been toying around with the idea of competing, maybe, someday—even running against Aaron Hill. It was April now. Hill was coming here in less than two months. Here to the Winter Sports Dome.

They hurried along the Dome's high concrete walls.

Sophie was telling him about her brother's visit. "And, Willis, he expected me to pack up and leave with him, just like that."

"You told him no, didn't you?" He kept his arm tight through hers. Sophie leaned her head against his shoulder. The wind gusted down the long bare walkways, and he zipped up the jacket of his new red nylon warmup suit. It was his birthday present from Sophie.

A troop of athletes came toward them, flying along with the wind behind them. The high hurdlers carried their long poles like furled flags. Men and women. They started down a flight of stairs to the team gate.

"They're so light on their feet," Sophie said.

"Let's go in with them." It was something he suddenly wanted to do. They hurried after the team and were almost the last ones past the guard. As soon as they were through the gate, Willis said jubilantly, "He thought we were part of the team. Did you see that, Soph? Did you see how easy it was?"

"What if he'd stopped us, Willis? What would we have done then?"

Willis laughed. "We would have paid." It wasn't the money he was thinking about. He didn't care about the money. It was how easily he'd melted into the team. If he'd stayed with them, he could have gone into the locker room and out onto the field, maybe even run as part of the team. "I fit right in," he said.

"It's your running suit," she said. "But how about me?"

"You're my trainer." It was half true, more than half true. Sophie had gone from just pacing him in the car out at the air base to recording his time and discussing what he had to do to make his time better. It didn't escape him that since Sophie had started coming out with him, his time had improved steadily. Just her being there had a lot to do with it.

He was no longer running for himself alone. He wanted to look good in Sophie's eyes and he wanted to look at those records and see them improving. It was satisfying. And then he thought that if he could improve this much with Sophie, how much more he would be capable of with some real competition.

In the stands, they found a place above the starting line. A seated row of judges was opposite them at a long table. "I've never been to a track meet before," Sophie said. "I've never been in a place like this before." She was looking up and around at everything. "It's like a giant bird cage."

Willis was excited, too. There was something about being here, with all these people, a sense of possibilities—maybe it was the size of everything, the scale, the height of the dome, the colors of all the different teams, the hawkers, the music, the banners. Maybe it was the noise and enthusiasm of the crowd, and the way the air vibrated and everything was brighter, larger and anything seemed possible. Even racing against Aaron Hill.

Aaron Hill. Was he actually thinking that? Him? In a race against Aaron Hill? That was competition. The real, the ultimate test. Crazy. Even if he was good enough, which he half doubted and half believed, how could he? He belonged to no team, was part of no organization, had no standing anywhere. Who would let him on the same track with Hill? Who was he that Hill would even want to or agree to race against him? It was simple out-and-out crazyness. But it didn't stop Willis from thinking about it.

"Who do I watch?" Sophie said.

"Watch green number twelve." The runners were lining up below them.

"Why him?"

"I like his looks."

The starter's gun popped. The race began. "Come on," Willis called to his runner. "Get on the inside."

"Come on, Twelve!" Sophie yelled.

Their man ended up fifth in a field of eight. "That bum," Willis said.

The women's events really interested Sophie, the vaulters and high jumpers especially. "They're flying," she kept saying to Willis. "I'm so glad I came."

Halfway through the meet, they went behind the stands to get something to eat. Sophie put a thin line of mustard on her hot dog. "Willis, I keep thinking you should be out there."

All the old remarks were ready to fall from his lips: He was a loner. He hated people watching him, knowing about him, asking questions. He ran because he loved to run, not to compete, not to get trophies. All true. But right now, his reasons sounded like excuses to him.

Why didn't he run in competition? Why didn't he race? He'd been scared in junior high, but he wasn't fourteen years old anymore. What did he have to be afraid of? All he could do was make a fool of himself. So what if people laughed? At least he'd know, once and for all, how good he was.

"You want me to go up against Hill when he comes here in June?" he said to Sophie. There! That was the idea he'd been sniffing around, poking at, circling around as if it were some large, unpredictable animal that he'd better not come too close to.

"Sure I do," she said, "and I'll come watch you."

"Will you?"

"You know I would."

"Well, maybe you'll be there, but you won't see me. You have to be in college to be eligible to run, which I'm not."

"What about people like you, people who are working and are so good and want to run?"

"There's always the running clubs, but I don't belong to them, either. I don't belong to anything, except me." That was what he always said. Then something happened that was a little eerie. Sophie reached right into his head and plucked out what he'd been thinking but didn't dare say.

"Never mind college. What if you just came here and ran? Who's going to stop you?"

"How about forty security guards and every runner in the Northeast?"

"They won't catch you. You're so fast you won't let them."

That animal, that other animal, the one inside him, that hungry one—Ambition—was on its hind legs now. It had reared up, eager and ready. Yes. Who could stop him? He'd come in running and never stop till he crossed the finish line.

They went back and watched the fifteen-hundred-meter race. Willis sat forward. "That's my event," he said. He watched intently, as if he were on the track himself. In his mind, he was there, running, in the pack, then moving up, taking the lead, breaking out. No one could stop him.

Nothing could stop him—not if he wanted to run. Not his not being in college, his not belonging—none of that would matter. And if he ran against Hill, nobody could deny him his place. Then they'd all know him.

At the end of the meet, after the awards ceremony, he and Sophie joined the crowds on the track. Only a few of the athletes remained. The judges were gone, their chairs kicked over. A kid ran across the top of the officials' table. Willis stood on the track, scuffed the surface, then went to the starting line and knelt down in the runner's position.

Thirty

Almost without admitting it to himself, Willis started serious training, as if he had made up his mind to enter the June Invitational, the one in which Aaron Hill was going to run. He had six weeks to get ready. "Enough time?" Sophie asked.

He didn't answer. He didn't want to think about that. If he thought about it, he would know there wasn't enough time, but six weeks was all he had.

He and Sophie worked out his training program. She bought a new notebook and wrote out the schedule. He had forty-two days. She gave a page to each day. Every day there had to be a mixture of long conditioning runs, speed training, wind sprints and uphill dashes. She checked off each routine as he completed it and entered the times. His goal was to work up to sixty miles of long-distance running every week.

At first he was a little anxious about his leg. It still got occasional twinges. But his leg was strong. He was feeling fine. Every day the running got better. Mornings, he ran his old route in the neighborhood, and after work, he went up to the college track. On the weekends, he and Sophie went to the air base, where they had laid out a quarter-mile straightaway. It wasn't your standard quarter-mile running track, but it gave him something to work against.

Sophie stood at the finish, holding the new stopwatch. When she raised a white handkerchief, he got ready. When it fell, he was off. At first his time was fair, not good, not good enough. He still needed a lot of work.

How could he enter a real race? He was deficient in so many ways. He'd never had coaching. He'd never had competition. Never run against a clock, didn't know how to start, how to conduct himself on the track. There were strategies to running; there were tactics, things to do that made a difference in a race. All he could do was get in the best condition possible and then go in there and run his heart out.

Sophie coached him and he coached himself. As he ran, he tried to visualize a real race, the other runners. What lane was he in? Who was in front of him? Who was behind him? Who was holding back? Who was gaining on him? When should he move to the inside track? When should he kick?

One night, he woke up in a sweat. He'd dreamed he was on the track with Aaron Hill. Willis was on the ground and Hill was looking down at him, his hands on his hips. The next day Willis went to the Y and added Nautilus training to his schedule. He'd fooled with it on and off before, but never consistently. Now he started working with the weight machines in earnest, an hour three times a week.

Each day, in between the running, there was the other

reality. Work. The factory. Indoors. The closeness. The heat. The blue oily fog over the machines, the foul air that was clogging his lungs. The pressure. Miholic yelling for him.

"Pierce! Clear the platform. . . . Pierce! get that unit outside. . . . Where's that special order you crated?" Pierce! Pierce! Pierce! Like the fans he'd dreamed of, on their feet and calling his name. Only it was Miholic.

"Do you think you'll be doing this for the rest of your life?" Willis asked Benny.

"Not me," Benny said.

"Maybe you'll go to college."

"Me? No way."

"What if you got a sports scholarship?"

"I don't think they give it in my sport," Benny said with a smirk.

"I might go to college someday," Willis said.

"You? What for? They're not going to make you any smarter. Only poorer."

After work, Willis began hanging around the university track. It was a busy place: Clumps of athletes—men and women jumpers, vaulters, shot-putters—working out, getting coached. Willis moved from one group to another, watching and listening. Nobody paid any attention to him. Some of the athletes wore the school's gold-and-black track outfits, but most of them were wearing the same kind of ragtag outfit he had on.

One day he slipped into a pack of runners. The black guy running next to him said, "I don't know what I'm doing here." He wore a green T-shirt and red cutoffs. "I've got a programming exam this week."

Willis nodded, as if he understood. When he saw the guy again a few days later, he said, "How'd the exam go?"

The guy gave him the thumbs-up sign.

In the same half-chancy way, Willis started participating in some of the field practices. It was riskier, because the coaches were here. One day he was near a group doing wind sprints. A coach called the runners up, six at a time. "One more," the coach said. There was an empty slot. "You." He pointed to Willis.

"Me?"

"Yeah, you. Get in here."

The other guys looked at Willis, but nobody said anything. He stood up and got into position. "Go!" the coach yelled, and they were off. Sixty meters. Willis finished in the middle. Maybe if he hadn't been so nervous he could have done better.

The coach beckoned him. "Keep your head up. You're running with your head down."

Running the next sprint he kept his head up, and he did better. The coach gave him a nod and called him over. "You always wear that hat?"

Willis took it off and put it into his pocket.

"Why haven't I seen you before? You're good. Are you on the team?"

Willis shook his head.

"Why not?"

"I work. I don't have a lot of time."

The coach looked annoyed. "I don't have time, either. I don't have time to waste on men who aren't serious." He was young, but when he took off his cap, his head was completely bald. He looked like an egg with eyes.

"I'm serious," Willis said.

"You must be a freshman. What's your name?"

"Willis Pierce."

"Spell that for me." He wrote it down. "You've got

potential, Pierce. I like the way you run. You want to let it go to waste, that's your business, but if you get out here every day, I can make a runner out of you."

This was the way it always happened in the stories: the coach picking the natural athlete out of the pack, the kid nobody knew or liked, or the kid who had this great natural talent but who never tried or didn't care, or maybe the kid who was too poor, and the coach telling him it was a sin to throw talent away. And at the end of the story the kid came through at the crucial moment, winning for the team and for the coach and for himself.

And for a moment, standing there, Willis was that kid.

And then he looked at the coach, at his fair, almost invisible eyebrows, at his smooth, eggshell face, and he heard the shouts and the coaches' birdlike whistles, and he heard the soft thud of feet on the track, and his heart dropped, because it wasn't a story, after all.

Thirty-One

That weekend was the first really hot day of spring. He and Zola and Sophie went to the beach. It looked like everybody in the city had had the same idea. There was a long line of cars waiting to get into the park, and the parking lot was packed. There wasn't a spot on the beach, either, and they had to settle for the grass farther back.

"Swim first?" Sophie said. She wore a pair of shorts over her swimsuit.

He put the leash on Zola and they went over to the shallow water. It was so crowded that people were just standing in the water.

He watched Sophie dunking herself in the water. "What'd I give you all those swimming lessons for, Sophie?" he yelled. She waved, pinched her nose and went under again.

When she came out, she said, "Why don't you go take your swim? I'll watch Zola."

Willis went to the end of the beach, to the diving platform. He dove off the diving board, then swam out beyond the ropes. A lifeguard patrolled nearby. Willis thought of what the track coach had said the other day. You've got potential, Pierce. He'd walked away, because what else could he do? But he'd been tasting the idea ever since, and he still hadn't gotten all the flavor out of it.

After he swam, he went looking for Sophie. She'd moved their stuff farther back, where there was a little shade. Sophie got the food out. She'd brought potato salad, soda and chips. He'd brought a couple of bagels and cream cheese. "This potato salad is good. Did you make it?" he said.

"Just like I made the gingerbread cookies. Thank Brenda."

"Does she know I'm eating it?"

"Oh, she likes you," Sophie said.

"It was a good thing I was in the car that day or she would have broken both my kneecaps."

"That's an awful thought."

"Me not able to run? Damn straight."

She passed him a can of soda. "My brother wrote me. He says they have to have me up there with the baby so close."

"What are they going to do if you don't show up? What if there's no Sophie? What then?"

She was sitting cross-legged, leaning toward him. "I was there to help Pat with both the other babies. I feel sort of guilty."

"Well, you told your brother you'd go up for a few days when she has the baby." He pushed the hair off her forehead. He loved the way she looked and the way he felt and the way they were together, and he wanted to tell her something good. "Want to hear something nice?" And he told her how the coach had called him aside and talked to him. "And then he said he could make a runner out of me."

"I told you," she said. "You've got talent."

"That's just what he said."

"Isn't that wonderful? You're always saying you're not sure. But this is proof." Her face was shining and she kissed him.

Later, they walked around the edge of the beach and ate potato chips. They walked arm in arm, slowly because of Zola. "This has been a really perfect day," Sophie said. "You're not going to feel bad because you didn't run, are you?"

"Everyone's got to take a day off now and then. Otherwise you get stale."

As they got closer to the concessions, the walk got more and more crowded. "Maybe we should go," Sophie said. "Do you want to take one last swim?"

"Maybe." He glanced over at the diving platform.

A girl was standing alone on top of the ladder. She was tanned, and her dark hair fell to her shoulders. She was wearing a white bikini, and the light coming off it seemed to surround her with a glistening haze. For a moment he thought it was Lee. She was like an actress or a dancer, someone perfect, too perfect to belong in this place. She stood on the platform, apart and above everyone else, then raised her arms and disappeared into the water.

"Willis?" Sophie passed her hand in front of his face. "Hello, in there. You didn't hear anything I just said."

"Yes, I did," he said. She'd asked him something about food. It was always food with Sophie. Suddenly everything bothered him. Sophie's talking about food again, and all these fleshy, naked people, and the smell of mustard and suntan lotion, and the way everyone was packed together like cornflakes in a box.

Was this all people did? Work and sleep and eat and eat and eat some more? He glanced up at the platform again. There were just a couple of kids up there, fooling around.

He wanted to move, take big steps, stride out of here, escape. Escape from himself. Escape from what he was thinking. His big news that he'd stored up to tell Sophie didn't seem like anything now, because it wasn't anything. When the coach had said, I can make a runner of you, it had felt like he'd handed Willis a bright, shiny trophy, but now it just seemed like a piece of tin in a Cracker Jack box.

Him, run? Against Aaron Hill? He'd been making believe all these weeks. The Mystery Runner. The outlaw coming from nowhere. Clark Kent at the racetrack. Superrunner. Superdope. Who was he? He was nobody. He was a laborer in a factory. Nobody was going to let him run in a college meet.

Famous? Race Aaron Hill? He was a dreamer, and that made him a fool.

He didn't intend to go back to the coach's practice, but later that week Sophie asked him about it. She had the workout book open and was bringing it up to date.

"I haven't been back," he said.

"Oh." She was surprised. "I thought you were going."

"I've been running." He wanted to let it go at that, but she kept asking questions, and he said he was going over tomorrow. He didn't feel like explaining how discouraged he'd begun to feel. He didn't want Sophie to know that he'd lost his spirit.

"Pierce," the coach said, "I've been looking for you." He flipped through a sheaf of papers. "I want to show you something." And he showed Willis his name on the roster. "Last name first. That's the way we do it. Pierce comma Willis." The coach looked pleased. He wanted Willis to show some enthusiasm. "I don't put everyone on this list. There's a little paperwork to be done and then we'll get you all set with a uniform and the rest of the stuff you need."

A little paperwork? Willis could imagine the coach in the front office, and the head honcho or the foreman or whoever they had there saying, Willis Pierce? Who's that? There's no Willis Pierce registered in this school. And the coach, with his round, sincere eyes, not getting it and saying it again. You've got to have his name. I was just talking to him. Pierce. Pierce comma Willis.

Thirty-Two

In the zoo, Sophie and Willis wandered around looking at the animals. "Look at the giraffes," Sophie said.

"Long legs," he said, but his mind was elsewhere.

"I love the zoo," she said. She put her arm through Willis's. "Look at the elephants. Don't they look like old, dusty blankets?" At the monkey cage, she pointed to a male sitting off by himself with his arms crossed. "Willis, who does he remind you of?"

"Your boss." It was the first time all morning that he laughed. Maybe the first time all week. It felt as if his face had cracked. He'd stopped running. Not a day since he'd seen his name on the coach's roster. And he hadn't told Sophie yet.

He'd been having bad dreams every night. Running dreams. The dreams would start beautifully. Him running through crowds, then running alone through the country, hearing only the whisper of his footsteps, seeing flowers and butterflies and the road rising and falling and climbing toward the sky.

Then, suddenly, the dream road tilted steeply down, and he could hardly keep his balance. Ahead, he saw a wreck, a burned hulk of a car on the side of the track. And his father coming toward him, his coat open, words coming out of his mouth that Willis couldn't hear or understand. And then he was tangled in the arms of his father's coat.

He cried out. He fought. He was being held and beaten. He fought back, but he had no strength. His knotted fists were soft as pillows. Every time he had this dream, he woke confused, unsure, depressed.

At the zoo's pavilion, they ran into Lee and Benny, both of them dressed in white and wearing dark glasses. They looked like they had come to the zoo to make a movie. They were the stars, waiting for the director. And what were he and Sophie? The extras waiting to walk on for the crowd scene.

Benny waved. "Willis! Over here."

"Oh, him," Sophie said. She made a face. Willis was reluctant, too, but they walked over.

"You remember Willis, don't you?" Benny asked Lee. "And this is, uh . . ."

"Sophie," Sophie said in a loud voice.

"Oh, right. Sophie," Benny said. "The shy and elusive Sophie." He had a camera around his neck, and under his white jacket he wore a black T-shirt that said TOGETHER WE CAN.

"Can what?" Sophie asked.

Benny looked down at his T-shirt and laughed. "Well, Sophie, I haven't figured that one out yet."

Willis and Sophie went to the counter to get something to eat. "Don't let me sit next to him," Sophie said.

"Okay," Willis said, but when they returned to the table, Lee moved over to make room for him and he sat down next to her. Sophie ended up next to Benny.

"Every time I come to the zoo, I see you guys," Benny said.

"No," Sophie said, "this is the first time we've been here."

"Same for us." Benny had a big smile on his face.

"Ooh! Funny." Sophie turned to Willis. "I fell for that."

"Your cone's upside down," Benny said.

She had a scoop of chocolate in a dish with the cone set on top of it. "That's the way I always eat my ice cream."

"Strange."

"You think so? My brother likes his with spaghetti."

"She's putting me on," Benny said, "isn't she, Willis?"

"All the time," Willis said. He swallowed a yawn. Benny could be a pain. Willis looked at Lee. She hadn't said anything, and the dark glasses made it hard for him to read her face. He thought of asking her about his seeing her on the diving board. Had it really been Lee?

He remembered the haze of light around the figure on the diving board. She had been distant, unreal, like a goddess in the sky. And now she was sitting next to him, her hand inches from his. Her hands fascinated him. She had a ring on every finger and glittery nails and gold chains on her wrists.

"Are you still running, Willis?" She pushed her dark glasses up into her hair.

"He runs every day," Sophie said proudly. "Don't you, Willy?"

He moved the ketchup and sugar jars around on the table. Sophie's voice jarred him with its eagerness.

"He runs twice a day and . . . how many miles this week, honey? Is it fifty? He's running up at the college, too. The coach is working with him."

He shut his eyes. He wished she hadn't said that. "Still working in the market?" he asked Lee.

"Oh, yes," she said languidly.

"Since when are you running at the college?" Benny said.

Willis shook his head. "I just went a couple of times."

"No," Sophie said, "you're going every—"

Willis kicked her foot, and she stopped and just sat there.

For a moment, nobody spoke. Then Benny raised his camera. "Willis, turn to Sophie. Let me get a shot of you two. Move a little closer. Sophie, put your arm around your man."

Sophie hesitated, then slapped her hand on Willis's shoulder. "Hate you," she whispered in his ear. Then she smiled at Benny. "Is it one of those instant cameras?"

"It's a single-lens reflex."

Benny took the picture. Sophie moved away from Willis. "I don't know the first thing about cameras," she said to Benny.

"It's easy to use. All you have to do is adjust for the light and the focus. You see that little mark? Here, try it."

Willis watched them. Their heads were together. All of a sudden they were buddies. Why? Because Sophie was mad at him. When they were alone, he'd talk to her, tell her why he'd stopped going to the coach's practice. As a matter of fact, he'd say quietly, I'm not even running that much anymore. Nothing to get excited about.

He turned toward Lee. He imagined telling her the same thing. You're not running, Willis? she'd say. Oh. That was all she'd say. No surprise, no popped-open face, no Oh, why, Willy? She wouldn't ask him anything.

If he felt like it, he'd tell her about seeing his name on the roster and how, right after that, he'd stopped running. How all that talk about running and racing and becoming famous just stopped meaning anything to him. The whole idea had been like a big, bright balloon that someone had poked a finger into and the balloon had burst.

Fine. Nothing to get excited about. He was possessed by a what-do-I-care? attitude. He was who he was. Willis Pierce, who worked in a factory. What did running have to do with that? What was running going to get him? College boys ran to get their exercise. They were the ones who got the awards and the trophies.

He was aware of himself, relaxed, sitting there in the sun, turned toward Lee. Lee, he'd say, now that I'm not running, I'm free. I can do anything I want, go anywhere. I don't have to be working all the time. So what do you say? I have a car, a little money, we could take a trip. Just you and me. No fuss. Just get in the car and go.

He imagined the two of them in the car, Lee in front next to him, Zola in back. He was driving, it didn't matter where. He'd seen a movie like this once. He couldn't remember the name. The man and the woman driving through the country on a curving road with trees and bushes.

"Do you like to drive?" he asked Lee.

"Yes. I'm a good driver."

And he imagined the road rising and him driving and her beside him. And then sometimes she was driving and he was in the seat next to her, not thinking, just watching the road unfold in front of them.

Thirty-Three

When they walked over to the pony and camel rides together, Sophie was next to Willis. But so was Lee. He was actually walking closer to Lee than to Sophie. Was she being too sensitive? She didn't think so. Willis had been in a mood all morning, but they'd been having a pretty good time till they ran into Benny and Lee.

Well, if they ran into them, they could run away from them, too. She took Willis's arm, gave it a little squeeze and a tug, but there was no response. His arm was like a piece of wood.

"Get up on the camel, Lee," Benny said. "I want to take a picture of you on the camel."

"It's too high. I'm not dressed for this."

"Lee, don't be a baby. It'll make a great shot." He didn't let up. "I want it for our album. Come on, you love to have your picture taken."

"Not on a camel."

"Be a good sport, angelface."

"Benny!" She turned to Willis. "Willis, talk to your friend. Make him stop it."

"Don't you think we should go?" Sophie said to Willis. She didn't want to be around when other people were fighting, but Willis just gave her a blank look.

Benny got his way, and Lee got up on the camel. "Can't you make it hold still?" she said to the pony boy.

"Willis." Sophie shook his arm. He couldn't take his eyes off the beautiful Lee.

"Benny, take the picture before I fall off." The camel was shifting around. "Where's the brake on this thing?"

"Lean back. Show a little leg."

"Forget it. I'm getting off right now. You're all done, Benjamin."

"Wait, a couple more shots."

Just then, the camel started to move. Lee grabbed the pommel. The camel trotted down the path, Lee rising and falling like a boat on the water.

"Hang on, honey!" Benny called. "Hey," he said to the pony boy, "stop that thing."

"Don't worry," the pony boy said, "Abdul will just go around the track and come right back."

"Lee's not going to fall off," Sophie added. The camel was like Ferdie, a big, slow farm horse they used to have. He was so big and so gentle, Sophie could walk under him without fear.

The pony boy ambled after the camel. He wasn't worried. He knew his camel. So what was Willis doing, running past him down the track and blocking the camel? The fireman with his net out. The rescue squad. The good guy, saving the princess. If she had been up there, Sophie thought, Willis would have fallen asleep.

He ran around the side of the camel and held his arms up to Lee. "It's okay, I'm here."

The way he was looking up at Lee made something hard stick in Sophie's throat. He was glowing. Sophie knew that face. It was a face only she should see. That face belonged to her. To them, when they were together. He didn't have the right to give it to anyone else. It was a private face, a special face.

She dug her hands into her pockets. She felt like crying, but she just stood there watching as Lee slid off the camel and into Willis's waiting arms.

Thirty-Four

"Where's Sophie?" Lee said.

"She probably went to the little girls' room," Benny said.

Willis didn't say much. He hung around Lee, a little dazed, still feeling her arms around his neck. It was crazy. He should have been thinking about Sophie. One minute she was there and the next she was gone. He should have gone right after her. If he'd been thinking—but he hadn't been thinking.

The three of them drifted over toward the women's room. Lee went in to check and came out shaking her head. They walked toward the gate. Maybe Sophie was waiting there.

Going past the pony and camel rides again, Benny said, "How about a camel ride, angel?"

Lee threw her arms around Willis. "Save me!" she whispered into his ear. "My boyfriend's in love with a camel. Let's escape."

For the second time, Willis's arms were around her. He smelled her skin, her hair. Her lips were next to his ear. Benny framed another shot of the camel.

"Hey, boyfriend," Lee said, "meet you at the gate." She put her arm through Willis's. That was the way they were when Lee spotted Sophie at the bus stop across the street from the zoo. "There she is, Willis."

Willis waved his free arm. Sophie didn't wave back.

"Uh-oh, you've got troubles," Lee said.

He crossed the street. Sophie was on the bus already, and he followed her in. She was sitting next to a child with a huge blue-and-white panda in his arms. Willis stood next to her. "Sophie, I was looking for you."

"I noticed." She patted the panda. "Did you win it?" she said to the little boy.

"My mommy won it." He looked around to see if his mother was still sitting behind him.

"Sophie, what happened?"

"Ask Lee." She said it without looking at him.

"What are you talking about?"

"Oh, you know!" She began drumming on her leg. "The camel! Lee! How would you feel if I went running after Benny?"

"He wasn't on the camel."

"Very funny."

"It didn't mean what you think," he said.

She looked at him. "You can't say one thing and think something else, Willis. It gives you a crooked look."

"Is that Brenda talking?"

"Don't you even know me? Can't you even hear what I'm saying? Forget it." She stroked the panda. "I don't want to talk to you right now. I don't want to talk to you, period. Why don't you go your way and I'll go mine?"

He went to the back of the bus and sat down. What was he doing on this bus? His car was at the zoo. Thanks a lot, Sophie. He glared at the back of her head, ordered her to turn around and look at him.

When the little boy with the blue panda got off the bus, Willis went forward and sat with Sophie. She looked at him. "Hi," he said.

She didn't answer.

"You're mad at me," he said.

"Brilliant!"

"Why should you be mad at me?" he said. She wanted him to be something he wasn't. What if he said he'd never look at another girl? It would be a lie. "Guys look. Girls do, too. Don't tell me you don't look. You made such a big thing of not liking Benny, but you cozied right up to him."

"Different!" she said. "Benny? I'd never choose him over you."

"I didn't choose Lee. I caught her when she fell off the camel. If you fell off a camel, I'd catch you. Did you see me do anything else?"

"You didn't just catch her. You know you didn't. I saw your face."

"I know I wasn't in the greatest mood."

"What's mood got to do with it? I know about your mood. I didn't mind that. You hurt me, Willis. You acted like I wasn't important to you. Sometimes you act like you care and sometimes you act like you wish I'd disappear."

"No," he said. He started to answer, then he shut up. Why? Because it was true? No, it wasn't true, but it was almost true. "I'm moody sometimes, but even when I'm moody, I'm glad you're there," he began, but then he couldn't go on. "I can't be making speeches all the time," he ended lamely.

"I'm not talking about speeches. I'm not talking about moods. I'm talking about us." She was speaking very softly and there were tears in her eyes. "You didn't want me, Willis. You wanted her."

She didn't say anything else, and at the next stop he pulled the cord and got off the bus and walked the rest of the way home.

Later, at home, he fed Zola and watched some TV just to have something to look at. Finally, he had to get out. He told himself that if he ran, he'd feel better, but he didn't run. He wandered around for a while downtown, noticing all the couples, making himself feel good and miserable; then he went home.

The next couple of days he didn't try to make up with Sophie. When he went to work, he walked by the newsstand. He didn't stop, he didn't say anything, but he looked over, gave her a hurt look. She saw him and she didn't say anything, either. She didn't want him.

This person he saw across the street wasn't the person he knew, not the Sophie who worked at the newsstand and didn't know her way around the block. This wasn't somebody waiting for him in the doorway, somebody who was eager and glad to see him. This was somebody he didn't recognize. The way she stood there, the cool way she looked over at him—everything about her said, Who are you? What do you want? What are you doing here?

The hell with her, he thought. He stayed away, didn't go to her house, didn't even go get his car, which was still parked up near the zoo. Maybe if he left it there long enough, they'd tow it away and he'd have to pay a big fine to get it back. It was just one more lousy thing to think about.

He kept going over and over their fight. Sophie. The zoo. The camel. Lee and Benny. Then back to Sophie. Lee and Sophie. Lee like a movie star and Sophie like, well, Sophie. Being around Lee, how could he not look at her? She was beautiful. Sure, he'd liked it when she'd fallen into his arms. He'd liked rescuing her. So what? He was a rescuer. He'd rescued Zola and he'd rescued Sophie, and now Lee.

Thursday was a lousy day. He had to wait around for an hour for work and it made him nervous. He began to think that there was no work and the job was coming to an end. And where would he get another job? Being fired would fit in with everything else that was happening to him. Miholic finally stuck him on a job with Vinnie and Wolpe, old molasses and glue themselves.

Friday, he couldn't stand his misery anymore and he stopped by the stand. "Have you got my copy of *Runners' World*?"

"No," she said. She'd changed her hair. She had a green scarf around her shoulders. She looked cool, pale and distant. She turned to another customer and didn't come back to Willis.

Thirty-Five

Monday, on the way to work, he scratched on the side of the newsstand, like Zola announcing herself. "Zola says hi, Sophie," he said. A kid popped out, a blotchy-faced boy he didn't recognize. "Who are you?" Willis said. His face got hot. "Where's Sophie?"

The kid didn't know anything about any Sophie. All he knew was that Carl picked him up this morning and told him he was working here for now.

"Sophie Browne. Where is she? Did Carl put her at another stand?"

The kid didn't know anything.

"When's Carl going to be here?" The kid didn't know that, either.

After work that day, Willis went over to Sophie's house. In the parking lot, four little girls were skipping rope. Brenda's kid, Jessie, was with them. "A my name is Anna and I come from Alabama," a girl sang. "My boyfriend's name is Andy and he really is an actor."

He went inside and knocked on Sophie's door. What was he going to say to her this time? Sophie, I'm sorry. I was wrong. Let's not fight. Or, if we're going to fight, let's fight and get it over with.

"Sophie?" He knocked again. Then he went downstairs and knocked on Brenda's door.

"Sophie's not here," Brenda said.

"Where is she? When's she coming back?"

"She went home," Brenda said coolly.

"Home?"

"Uh-huh." She started to shut the door.

"Hey, wait! What's going on here? Stop jerking me around, Brenda. What do you mean, she went home?"

"She went home, that's what I said."

"To the farm?"

"Uh-huh."

"Did she leave a message for me?"

"No."

"How'd she go?"

"Her brother came and got her."

"Floyd? When?"

"This morning."

"She left this morning?" He wasn't getting it. He didn't want to get it.

"That's what I just said."

"Is that all? She didn't even leave me a message? Nothing for me? Did she say when she was coming back?"

"She said she'd let me know." Brenda closed the door.

He knocked again. "Did Pat have the baby?"

She opened the door a crack. "Not that I know about." Then she couldn't contain herself. "She went to get away from you. And after what she told me, I don't blame her."

He went outside and sat down on the stoop, where the

kids were skipping rope. He was stunned. All this time he'd thought, okay, Sophie was mad, but she was here. It was just a matter of time.

How had things gotten this bad? He sat there, taking deep breaths, feeling worse and worse. She was gone. Sophie was gone.

He didn't go to work the next morning. He took Zola and went out. No place special, just walking. When he got hungry, he stopped to eat. Later, he was in the park. He didn't know how he got there. It was like a summer day. There were people everywhere, sitting in the sun and lying on blankets on the grass. Didn't anybody work? He went down to the pond, where he'd seen Sophie that day, where everything had really started. He remembered how happy he'd been.

Willis walked around. He knew Sophie wasn't there, but he kept looking for her. Near a stone wall, a photographer was taking pictures of a model in a fur coat. A man in white coveralls was arranging her hair, and a woman adjusted the coat. Zola ran right into the picture. "Take, take!" the photographer cried.

On the far side of the field there was a crowd listening to some musicians. The drummer was a skinny black man with a white goatee. A girl in a purple sunsuit was dancing alone on the grass. From a distance, the triangle player looked like Sophie. Maybe it was Sophie.

The closer he got, the more she looked like Sophie. She wore baggy pants and her hair jetted out in spikes. She was half turned away, her eyes closed, swaying and playing the triangle.

"Sophie," he said under his breath. "Is it you?"

He knew it wasn't Sophie, yet he felt it could be her.

He wanted it to be her. Hey, Sophie, he'd say to her, Brenda told me you left. Am I glad you didn't go. Am I glad to see you. Then he'd tell her again he was sorry. Really sorry. He never thought the fight would go on this long. And she'd say she'd missed him, too. And they'd kiss and everything would be good again.

The music ended, the players drifted away and the girl who looked like Sophie came toward him.

It wasn't Sophie. Not just the hair. Everything about her—not Sophie.

There was only one Sophie, and she was gone. He'd lost her. And it hurt so much that he knew he loved her.

He loved her.

It was the first time he'd ever said it. He loved her, and she was gone. It was as if everything that had ever been between them had disappeared, too.

It was like the music. Before you heard it, everything was ordinary. Then you heard the music and you went toward it and you saw the players and people dancing and you felt like dancing and you were happy and you thought the music would never stop. And then it did. The music stopped and there was nothing but you, sitting alone on a park bench, talking to yourself.

He started running again, running and training, doing everything he'd done before. He didn't think he was going to do it. He didn't plan it. He just woke up the morning after the park and went out and ran. It was like calling Sophie back to him.

He talked to her as he ran. See, Sophie, I'm running again. Nothing's changed. One stupid remark shouldn't change everything. Or one stupid afternoon.

He was running as well as he ever had, maybe better.

Running hard, more intensely, and with some recklessness. He wasn't holding back. He wanted the pain. He was in pain. Only when he ran did the pain go away. When he ran he believed Sophie was coming back. When he got home he thought he'd find her waiting for him, like that day when it was raining and she'd come with the cookies.

He started dreaming and thinking about the Invitational Race. The Aaron Hill race. One night he dreamed that he was on the starting line and his shoelaces broke. He knotted them and they broke again. He looked into the crowd. Somebody was there. He kept looking. And waiting. Looking for somebody he couldn't find.

He woke up and knew the dream was about Sophie.

Sometimes Zola gave him a puzzled look. Something was missing in her life, too. She'd get her paws up on his knees and look into his eyes. Where's Sophie?

Every day, every place he went, he looked for her. When he went by the newsstand, there was that lift, that moment of anticipation. She was going to be there and she'd give him that smile she always gave him, and everything would be the way it was before.

And then she wasn't there. She was never there.

Thirty-Six

You go your way, I'll go mine.

The morning of the race, Willis woke up with that phrase in his head. You go your way, I'll go mine. Sophie wasn't coming back. He rolled over and pulled the pillow over his head. An awful, sick feeling spread through him. You go your way. Her way was to leave him, to go back to the farm. And his way? What was it? Was he going to race? He didn't know anymore and he didn't want to think about it. He just wanted to do something to make the sick feeling go away.

He got up, made Zola's breakfast, made himself eggs and toast and then couldn't eat it. He flipped on the TV to get his mind off the race and watched cartoons. Would Sophie be at the Dome? Would she remember what day this was?

He scratched Zola's head, then teased her, held her muzzle. Zola raised her white eyebrows, her forehead wrinkled. Why? She seemed to say. Why are you doing this? She fought him, broke free and grabbed his wrist with her hot, wet mouth.

What if Sophie was at the Dome and he wasn't?

He crossed the room. Zola followed him with her eyes. He saw the Dome, saw the track and the stands, saw Sophie there, looking for him. Waiting for him. He knew she was going to be there and he had to be there, too.

He got dressed. He put on a pair of black running shorts with a gold stripe and a gold mesh, sleeveless jersey. He pinned the number 19—his age—on the back of the jersey, then pulled on the nylon warm-up suit that Sophie had bought him. He put his track shoes in a paper bag.

Before he left, he glanced at the Aaron Hill poster and his whole stomach heaved. He washed his mouth out and brushed his teeth again and put on his white Raleigh racing cap.

At the Dome he bought a general admission ticket. He didn't think about what he was going to do. He'd stopped thinking. He was just doing it.

There was a good crowd, but not a sellout. He didn't see Sophie anywhere. He took a seat not far from the judges' table. He kept looking around for Sophie. The Hill race, the men's fifteen hundred meters, was scheduled for later in the morning. He stood up. If she was there, she'd see him. He even waved, but then he felt foolish and sat down.

The judges, timekeepers and reporters shared one long table. The State U coach who'd talked to him was with his star runners. Bonner and Klein would do well, Willis thought, but neither one could take Aaron Hill.

He watched the relay races and saw a few runners he recognized. The black guy he'd talked to at practice ran the final leg. His team lost.

Willis found it hard to concentrate. His mind was on fast forward, jumping to that moment when he would enter the race. The first few seconds would be critical. When the gun went off, he'd be behind every runner. He'd be alone, vulnerable, easily picked off. To stay in the race, to even get into the race, he had to hurl himself forward, throw all his energy into those first moments. Timing was everything. If he started too soon, if he jumped in before the gun went off, they might scratch the race. And if he was too slow, if he didn't leap forward and get solidly into the pack fast enough, they'd grab him, pick him off like a bad egg.

There were six runners. He would be the seventh. His mouth was dried out and he kept swallowing. He picked out the point where he'd have to be when the race began.

"The next race will be the men's fifteen hundred meter." The announcement came over the PA system and then they started calling off the runners and their schools. Willis put on his track shoes and shoved his other shoes into the paper bag. He left his seat and went down to the row of seats closest to the track.

A couple of guards were chatting near the gate that he had to enter. He walked toward them. One of the guards looked at him. Willis nodded to him. "Good luck," the guard said.

When Aaron Hill came out from the lockers, there was a ripple of applause. He was wearing gold around his neck and on his wrist. Willis wiped his hands on his pants. You only had to look at Hill to see that he was a champion.

Willis kept his back to the coach and started stretching out. The runners were moving toward the starting line. Aaron Hill passed him and took his starting position. Willis took off his warmup suit and threw it onto the benches.

He knelt down and tied and double-tied his laces. He held his cap under his arm. He was sweating and his hands were shaking.

Again he looked up into the stands. High up, something red flashed. He moved along the edge of the track. The starter raised the gun. The runners leaned forward on their arms, one leg thrust back. The gun went off. The runners sprang away. Willis jammed his hat on his head and leaped onto the track after them.

He was alone too late. The runners seemed a great distance away from him. How had they gotten so far ahead of him? A man was waving ferociously at him from the side. Willis sprang away. Another man grabbed at him. He veered, ducked, then plunged after the runners. The numbers on their backs were black and as large as placards.

A runner with a bristly ginger-colored mustache turned and showed Willis his teeth, then shoved him aside.

Willis stumbled, kept running. He passed a green-and-yellow jersey, then another. He swung in behind a man with a black-and-gold shirt. He was safely in the pack.

Thirty-Seven

"This is Andy Lipski at WIBB, broadcasting from the Dome. Something extraordinary has just happened. The runners in the fifteen hundred meters are off to a fast start, but now there's a disturbance on the track. A runner, looks like one of the State University athletes, just came from the outside and swerved in between Parsky and Sanderson. Looks like Parsky swung at him. An official just ran out on the track. I've never seen anything like this before. Holy cow!

"That runner there doesn't belong. The officials are trying to get him off, but he keeps eluding them. . . . Bear with me, please, I've never seen anything like this before. The intruder, he's got a white cap on. He just jumped in when the race started. There were six runners, now there're seven. That's not a school uniform he's wearing! I see it now. This guy bolted in! I confess I didn't see it happen, but that's what it must have been. He's right in there with the pack. The officials are trying to head him off and not stop the race, but they can't get him. He's in there, in the middle of the pack. Do the lead runners know? I don't think they do, folks! Hill, Bonner and Robinson—they're just running their race.

"Holy cow, someone just tried to tackle this guy. I thought they had him, but he just sprang up like a deer and jumped over him. He's running down the track like he's doing the hurdles. He's not wearing anybody's colors. He's got a number on his back, but it's not on the program. He's nobody I recognize. It's somebody who bolted in from the stands. There's no way they can get him now without stopping the race.

"He's wearing a white cap. Did I say that? I don't believe this. The cap looks like a biker's cap. I have a feeling he's in the wrong race. He could be scheduled for another race and got in here by accident. But I don't think so.

"But he's a runner, folks—holy cow, they just tried to reach in again and yank him out. They can't touch him. He's slippery. He slipped right out of their hands. I've never seen . . . in all my years in broadcasting, this is a first.

"They've come around the first lap. He's still in there, still solid in the pack. He can run, folks. The judges all have their heads together. I thought they were going to stop the race, but they're letting it go on. It's a good race. It's tough. Blistering. Up front, it's Robinson, then Bonner and Hill. And then it's Sanderson, then the mystery runner, he's hanging in there! Parsky and Ciotti in back.

"The officials are letting the race continue. The guards have given up trying to eject the mystery runner. They're all watching and waiting. How long can he keep this up? This is an unfortunate event. I'm sure he's upset the runners he's with, but it isn't affecting the front-runners. Up front, it's still Robinson, then Bonner, then Hill on the inside, right on Bonner's heels.

"Behind them, Sanderson is moving up to a strong fourth position. It looks like a strong race. Would you believe that the mystery kid is still in fifth place? That's right. He's running stronger than Parsky and Ciotti. I have a feeling he could pass Sanderson if he moved to the inside, but then the officials could yank him out. He's keeping to the middle of the track. I've never seen anything like this in all the years I've covered track events.

"As we go into the backstretch of the third lap, Hill has moved up in front of Bonner. It's Robinson in front, Aaron Hill second and Bonner third as we go into the bell lap. Sanderson is moving up. The mystery kid is right with him.

"Somebody is running out onto the track again! One of the other athletes! He just tried to tackle the mystery kid! The kid ducked. He's lost his hat! He's still running. He just went past Sanderson. I can't believe this. Holy cow! The kid is in fourth place. He's just not going to be touched. I've never seen anything like this.

"Aaron Hill has just taken the lead. He and Robinson are neck and neck. This is the race everyone predicted. I don't think the lead runners are aware of the kid. Now Hill is pulling away and the mystery kid is still in there, folks. This is like a fairy tale. He's going by Bonner! I can't believe this. He's going by Bonner! Holy cow! He's in third place! It's Hill, then Robinson, then the mystery kid. I tell you whoever he is, he can run.

"Hill is opening up a couple of strides in front. The kid is right on Robinson's heels. He's passing him! I don't believe this! I can't believe what I'm seeing! These are the best runners in the East. Who is this kid? Somebody ought to recruit him. This is unbelievable.

"They're on the final stretch and it's the kid and Aaron Hill. Robinson's fading, but the kid is getting stronger. He's giving Hill a run. This is great! But it's Hill's race. He's taking charge now. He's going for it. Pulling away. He's all by himself. The kid is behind him. He's trying. Whoever he is, he's got guts. He's running his heart out. He's in there. He's in the race. And he's drawing up! He's coming up on Hill. I don't believe this! He's coming up on Hill. A stride separates them. They're on the last turn! They're coming up on the line! He's still fighting! It's close, it's close, it's close . . .

"It's Hill's race! He's won! The mystery kid is second! He's down. He's on his back. He's hurt. Officials are swarming all around him. I don't envy him.

"The cameramen are running. The guards have the kid. They've got him on his feet. He's swinging his arms. Looks like he's in pain. They're holding him up. They've got his arms stretched out. Two guards have him. He must have been running on pure guts at the end, because right now, folks, he looks like he's out of everything.

"The guards are all around him. They're pushing through the cameras and the reporters. They're dragging him off. Holy cow, did you ever see a race like this before? Did I say Aaron Hill won the race? It's not his best time. I don't have the official time yet, but I don't think he broke his record, but it's damn good. He ran a good, strong race.

"And now the women's fifteen hundred meters is getting under way. Ginny Ozick of Villanova looks like the strongest contender in this race. . . ."

Thirty-Eight

They dragged Willis off the track. Dragged him, yanked him, pulled him apart. He was crazy, crying, legs useless, lungs on fire, dying.

They ran him, carried him mostly, to a room underground. A long, low, windowless room. A dressing room. They had him on a table. One guard was by the door. Two others were holding him down. He braced himself for a beating. They were going to work him over now. Talk. Who are you? Where are you from? What have you been drinking? Talk, jerk. It was the interrogation room. The room he'd seen a hundred times on TV, in the movies. The Gestapo, the KGB, the CIA.

Talk. . . . Your ass is mud. We're going to break your legs.

He shook. He was falling apart. His shoulders, his stomach, his whole body shook. His lungs felt like they'd been cracked open. He couldn't stop shaking. He heard someone moaning. It was him. He was moaning and crying.

What had he done? All he felt was pain and fear.

Someone handed him a towel. A white-haired guard said, "What's your name, son?"

He shook his head. He couldn't talk. His throat was scraped raw. He felt around for his cap, but it was gone.

Someone was banging on the door. "Channel Eight News. Open up. You got no right to keep us out. The public has a right to know. Open up."

The white-haired guard went to the door and opened it a crack. "Get back from there," he ordered. "Nobody's coming in here."

There was a little scuffle and then the cameramen and the reporters pushed in. They rushed at Willis. Flashbulbs went off. Mikes were thrust at him.

"Who are you? What's your name? What'd you do it for? Did you think you were going to beat Hill?"

Willis kept his head down. He wished he had his cap. Had he done it? Caught Aaron Hill? Run against the champion? Run equal with him?

"What happened? Did you run out of steam? Do you realize what you did? Do you know you came in second? Come on, fella, don't you want to say anything?"

Came in second? Had he done it? Passed Robinson, passed Bonner? Passed them. He had done it. It was the dream. He'd run with Aaron Hill. Did it, did it, the moment he'd dreamed of, never believed would be, step for step, shoulder to shoulder, breath for breath, his step and Hill's step.

The reporters kept throwing questions at him. "When did you get the idea to do this? You have a bet with somebody? You almost beat him, man. Do you think you could have taken him?"

He was numb. He couldn't talk. He was still in the race,

still running, still on the track, still looking into Aaron Hill's eye, that one eye, that huge, investigating, noncommittal eye. Aaron Hill seeing him, taking him in for the first time, seeing Willis, Willis Pierce, seeing him at his shoulder, the challenger, the newcomer, the stranger, the mystery runner.

And at that moment Willis had seen his hero real. Uneasiness crossed that princely face. Lines of strain. It was a moment, a second, less than a second, but in that moment Willis had seen fear on Aaron Hill's face.

And then the real race began. Aaron Hill kicked. He lengthened his stride and pulled away, but not far. Willis clung to him. Willis was spent, finished, everything had been burned out of him, the air sucked dry, his lungs turned to ashes, muscles dead. And still he ran.

Aaron and Willis. Now it was a race for blood and oxygen. He wanted to put a hand on Hill's shoulder, hang on to him. He was like a boxer blindly clinging to his opponent, trying to stay in the fight. Hanging on, counting, eyes closed, space collapsing.

"Were you scared? Are you scared now? Do you know what they're going to do to you? Come on, this is your chance to tell your story on TV."

Willis sat with his head forward, his mouth open, spit slowly drooling to the floor. The finish line, cinders biting into his palms, tasting dust, half rising, blind and insane with pain, flinging out his arms and falling across the finish line.

He lifted his head, shielding his face from the cameras. "Aaron Hill"—his voice cracked—"Aaron Hill is the greatest." And then it all came swirling in on him again. The race and what he'd done. Aaron Hill. Sophie. And who he was. He felt something break in him, his heart tear loose. And then he was crying again.

Thirty-Nine

There was a picture of Willis on the front page of the sports section. The caption read: "Police attempt to run agile youth off track." The picture showed Willis on the track with his cap coming off, leaping away from the guard.

Willis studied the picture. He didn't recognize himself. He looked older. His mouth was open and there were hollows in his cheeks. He carefully cut the picture out of the newspaper and pinned it to the Aaron Hill poster. Then he read the article.

> NEW TRACK RECORD SET IN BIZARRE RACE
> LOCAL RESIDENT MARS HILL WIN
>
> In a race marred by the bizarre entry of a spectator onto the track, Aaron Hill set a new indoor record at the Eastern Regional Indoor Track Meet, barely improving his former time by two tenths of a second. The intruder may have influenced the outcome. He entered the race only moments after it began, wear-

ing track clothes, cleats and a white cap. He ran the entire race, eluding all attempts to remove him from the track. At the end, he was still in the race, challenging Hill, the clear leader, and coming within a hairbreadth of winning.

The police have identified the intruder as Willis Pierce, a local resident, who graduated North Side High and is currently employed at the Spring Street Consolidated Conveyor plant. The city has no plans to prosecute, according to Chief of Police Otto Miller.

Miller said, "It's out of our jurisdiction. This is a case of trespassing, which the university can take care of."

University officials said they were considering legal action. "Pierce," Chancellor Garlen said, "not only interfered with the race, but he endangered the other athletes as well. This isn't the kind of thing we're going to smile about and forget. Athletes could have been hurt. Whether the record will be considered official is in some question. Athletes who've worked all year for this event had their performances marred. Their concentration was affected. This is not a laughing matter."

The athletes themselves had mixed reactions. Aaron Hill, the winner, wants the results to stand. "My race wasn't affected. I don't feel he hurt me. I didn't even know he was on the track till he was on my heels. I thought it was Bonner coming up behind me."

Ivor Sanderson, when asked if he had any sympathy for the intruder, said, "No. They ought to throw the book at him. He messed up my race. He jumped in front of me, he affected my timing and my concentration. He threw my race off."

Forty

Willis was lying on the mattress, reading the newspaper article again. If Sophie had been here, they would be talking over everything. That moment when it was him and Aaron Hill. Could he have won? She'd say yes. If he'd started with the others. If he'd had expert training. If he'd run other races. Yes, it could have been you, Willis, crossing the finish line first.

There was a knock at the door. He sat up. Sophie? His face flushed, he felt the heat in his eyes. He scrambled up. He hurt everywhere, his legs and chest, every breath he took hurt.

Zola grabbed the paper and dragged it across the room. "Zola! My article!" Willis got the newspaper away from her, then Willis tucked in his shirt and went to the door barefoot.

It was sour Don from downstairs with a woman. "Pierce!" Don smiled. "I brought this reporter to talk to you." Don gestured and bowed. "Bunny Fried, I want to introduce my neighbor."

The reporter held out her hand. "Sorry to barge in on you. I tried to call you, but you're not in the phone book. I'm a reporter for the *Herald*. Can I ask you a few questions?"

"About the race?"

She nodded.

He thought about Sophie reading the story about him. "Is this a story that's going into the paper?"

"Definitely, Willis. Can we talk now?"

Don lingered. "So, how's the dog, Willis?"

"She's okay," Willis said, and held the door open for him.

"If you need anything else, Bunny," Don said, "I'll be downstairs."

"Sure. Thanks." Bunny Fried perched on the windowsill and opened a notebook. "Well, Willis, what I've heard about the race makes you sound like a crazy sort of publicity-happy kid."

"I'm not a nut! Running is my life."

"You didn't strike me that way."

He pointed to his picture on the wall. "Did you take that picture?"

"That's not my paper. I work for the afternoon paper, Willis. I see you have Hill's picture. Is he your hero?"

"Yes."

"Don't you think what you did hurt him?"

"No."

"That's what people are saying, that he would have run a better race. What do you say? I want to hear your side of the story."

"I made him run. He had to run hard to win. I didn't hurt anybody's race. All I wanted to do was race against Aaron Hill."

"Why?"

"Why? Because Aaron Hill's the best."

"That's the only reason? You didn't want anything else? Publicity?"

"No. What do I care about publicity? I'm a runner. I've been training for this race. I run every day."

"So do I," she said. "Not that I'm putting myself in your class." She smiled at him. "You must have done a lot of training, but did you really think you could beat Hill?"

"I almost did."

"How do you account for that? Are you as good as he is?"

He shrugged. "He must have had an off day."

"I'm really curious, Willis. I've never heard of you. Nobody ever heard of you before. Where do you train? What club do you belong to? Who do you run with?"

He tapped himself on the chest. "I'm a running club of one."

"You run alone? Is that what you're saying?"

"Yes."

"What other races have you run in?"

He shook his head.

"None? You mean to say this is the first race you were ever in? Coach Wright seems to know you."

"Who's he?"

"Willis, he's the track coach here at the college. You must know him. He knows you. I can't believe he doesn't want you on his team."

"You mean the bald-headed guy? I ran for him a couple

of times. That's the university. I don't belong there."

"Oh, yes, you work in a factory, don't you? What do you do?"

"I'm in the shipping department. I box stuff."

"That's really interesting." She was scribbling. "Did you know you were this good? Who's your trainer?"

"I train myself." He thought of Sophie. "And a friend works with me. She's helped me a lot."

"She? Is she a runner, too?"

He looked down at his bare feet. "No." He got a glass of water. He'd been drinking water all morning.

"One more question, Willis. When you were in high school, didn't anyone scout you?"

"No."

"I don't understand that."

"I wasn't on the squad."

"It's such an amazing story. What're your plans now, Willis?"

He squatted down and pulled Zola against him. "No plans."

"Are you going to continue running?"

"Running is what I do. I'm a runner. Like Aaron Hill says, I was born to run. That's me."

"Are you going to do this again?"

"You mean another race against Aaron Hill?" He hadn't thought about it. Maybe he'd go everywhere Aaron Hill went and race against him. Follow him all over the country. People would be expecting him. The kid who jumped into the race.

"Aaron Hill's a great runner. I still don't believe I was in the same race with him."

After the interview, he went down to the Laundromat and called his parents. They didn't seem to follow what had happened. Willis on TV? Stories about him in the newspapers? What had he done? "Are you in trouble?"

At work the next day, he was a hero. Everyone wanted to talk to him about the race. Wolpe had his arm around Willis. "I was sitting in front of the TV and I see this crazy idiot. I said, Who's that jerk running out there? Then I saw that white cap. I yelled for my wife. I told her, That kid, I work with him. It was like that movie where Charlie Chaplin, or Harold Lloyd or somebody, is locked out of his house and he's on the street in his underwear, looking for a barrel to hide in, and these runners come by and they're all wearing underwear, just like him, so he jumps in with them. Is that the way you did it, Willis?"

Vinnie pushed in. "You had that race, Pierce. You had it dead to rights. What'd he do, trip you? They should have disqualified him. I saw him. He gave you the shoulder, didn't he?"

"Willis is famous," Wolpe said. "Hey, you guys, we got a celebrity here in the shipping department."

Someone made a crown out of a paper bag and popped it onto Willis's head. He pulled it off and held it in his hand. Then a couple of guys from the paint department, who were musicians and played at weddings, talked to him about joining them. They showed him their card:

ARCHY AND BINOCCI, GUITAR AND ACCORDION. LIVE, AFFORDABLE MUSIC FOR YOUR BIRTHDAYS, WEDDINGS AND BAR MITZVAHS.

"I don't play an instrument," Willis said.

"We'll show you. It's easy."

There was a lot of kidding till work started. Even then some guys were still hanging around, looking at him, until

Miholic came out of his office. But even Miholic was curious. "Where'd they take you? The TV station?"

Benny didn't say anything to Willis, but all morning he kept looking at him. Finally, he said, "I can't believe you're a TV celebrity. Lee and I were watching the TV when we saw you."

"She was with you?" Willis said.

"You should have heard her scream. 'That's Willis!' Hey, man, I was screaming, too. I wanted you to win that race. Oh, did I want you to beat that guy. That would have made my day. You know those kids in college, everything's handed to them. I still don't know how you did it. That was fantastic. That was the most beautiful thing I ever saw."

In her column the next day, Bunny Fried devoted her whole column to Willis. She wrote about Willis as a jewel in the rough. "We have talent in our town that's untapped. What's a physical genius like Willis Pierce doing working in a factory? Think about that, Coach Wright."

Forty-One

Miholic called Willis into the office. "There's a phone call for you. From Dean Cummings's office."

"Who?"

"State University. They want to talk to you."

"Me?" As if he didn't know. The university was coming after him. They knew him, they knew where he lived, they knew where he worked. He'd broken their rules and now they were going to get theirs back. He didn't know what they could do to him, but everything he thought of was bad.

On the phone, a woman said, "Mr. Pierce, this is Mrs. Byrd, Dean Cummings's secretary. The dean would like to talk to you in his office. Could you come in today?"

"I work all day," he said.

"How about late this afternoon? Is five o'clock all right for you?"

"Is five thirty all right?" That would give him time to go home and clean up.

When he walked into the dean's office later that afternoon, there were three men waiting for him. It was a small office. The dean was behind his desk and the other two men were sitting against the wall, facing him. The only one he recognized was Coach Wright. None of them looked happy to see him.

The dean stood up and shook Willis's hand. "Mr. Pierce. Sit down."

The three of them sat in a line facing the dean. Willis put his hands in his pockets, then took them out, then finally sat with them clasped on his knee. He felt like he'd been called to the principal's office.

"How old are you?" the dean asked.

"Nineteen."

"When did you graduate high school?"

"Last year."

"Were you a good student?"

"I was okay."

The dean picked up a newspaper clipping from a folder on his desk. It had Willis's name on it. "And you work in, ah . . ." He adjusted his glasses. "Here it is. Consolidated Conveyer, Spring Street division. Is that right?"

"Yes." He wished the dean would get to the point. They were going to do something to him. Could they really put him in jail?

"What do you do there, Willis?"

"I'm in the shipping department." He wiped his hands on his pants.

The man he didn't know leaned toward him. "Willis! Okay if I call you Willis?" He had bushy eyebrows and sags under his eyes. "Are you really running sixty miles a week?"

"Pretty close."

"Every week? You never slack off?"

Willis sat up uncomfortably. "I try not to."

"What else?" the man said.

Willis told him about the hill training and the Nautilus and running at the air base. And all the time he felt like he was in first grade and being quizzed. Did he wash behind his ears this morning? Did he brush his teeth?

"Is there anything else?"

Willis shook his head.

Coach Wright didn't say anything. The dean shuffled through the folder.

Here it comes, Willis thought.

The dean sat forward. "I think you know why you're here, Mr. Pierce. The university doesn't like the way you did things. We seriously considered taking legal steps. The university can't run an organized sports program and allow any Tom, Dick or Harry to disrupt it at his own whim." He paused.

Willis wondered if he should say something. "I—" He cleared his throat.

"What you did is a dangerous precedent. What are we going to do, let excited fans run onto the field and tackle the players? Grab the ball? Run with it?" His voice rose. "If we let you get away with it, is that going to be a green light for every young, hotheaded kid?"

"I'm sorry," Willis said. It sounded lame. He didn't believe in excuses, but what else could he say? He had done it. He couldn't undo it. He hadn't thought about any of this stuff. He hadn't thought about anything but the race. Nothing. Nothing but running against Aaron Hill.

"There are ways to do things, and your way is not the right way."

"I'm sorry," he said again.

"Yes, I'm sure you are," the dean said.

There was a pause. The dean looked at the other two men. "Would you like to start, Coach Wright?" the dean said.

Willis pulled himself up and sat rigidly. Here it comes, he thought. Here it comes.

"We've been talking about you," Coach Wright said. The other man rubbed his hands together. They were all looking at Willis.

"We're prepared to offer you a full athletic scholarship," the coach said. "That would be tuition plus room and board and a small stipend."

"We'll expect you to enroll in the fall and start classes with everyone else," the dean said.

Willis looked around. Was the coach laughing? There was a smile on the other man's face. Was this some kind of weird joke? Why would they offer him a scholarship? There was a catch to it somewhere.

"It's rare to run into someone with so much natural talent," the dean said. "Isn't that right, Coach Wright?"

"Don't think it's going to be easy," the third man said. "You have to keep up with your classes. This is an honor and an opportunity. I went to this school. I graduated in fifty-two. You're being given an opportunity, young man. It's an honor. Don't abuse it."

"You say you train hard," Coach Wright said. "I'm going to train you a lot harder. I'll expect you out for every practice. And no excuses. And I want to talk to you sometime soon about starting training. We're not waiting until next fall."

Willis felt around for his cap. He missed it. Did they have it? Somehow the cap seemed realer than the offer. He wanted to ask for it, but the idea of asking for an old biking cap when they were offering him four years of college paralyzed him.

Four years of college. Free. Better than free, because they were going to let him run. He thought about running, wearing the uniform, belonging to the university. Running every day. Being on the same team with Bonner and Klein, the three of them racing each other. And maybe running against Hill again. Just the thought of it dried his mouth out.

Could he believe it? Had they really said that? Him in college? Nobody in his family had ever gone to college. He was the first one to even graduate high school. "I don't have the money," he said.

"Maybe you didn't hear me," the dean said. "It is a little sudden, I'm sure. It's a full scholarship. It pays everything. Room, board, books, fees, everything. We even provide you with an allowance, a modest stipend."

Could he do it? He wasn't worried about the running, but was he smart enough? He thought about all the kids in high school, the brains, the ones who ran the school, the ones who went to college. The ones someone like him never hung out with.

The dean stood up. "You're fortunate to have a gift. A gift is a blessing and a responsibility."

"Young man," the alumnus said, "don't forget, if you'd lost that race, we wouldn't be here talking to you."

"Nothing succeeds like success," the dean said, and he and the other men laughed.

Willis was still in a daze when he left. He walked out of the office and the moment he was out of the building he ran, flew down the street. Wait till Sophie hears this, he thought. She'll never believe it! And then he remembered.

Forty-Two

Monday he stayed home, waiting for Sophie. Tuesday he was famous. Wednesday, he was famous. Thursday, he got the college offer. Friday, he woke up with his eyes wet. Sophie.

Sophie again. And again.

And again, Sophie.

At work they had something new to talk about. Fourteen guys at Southern Cable had won the two-million-dollar lottery.

"They stayed with it for three years," Wolpe said. He tapped his head. "Smart! They knew they were going to win. They didn't get discouraged. They hung in there and they won. Two million bucks. Is it worth a buck a week?" He was organizing a pool. "Okay, who wants in? Twelve guys, a buck a piece every week and we stay with it till it happens. And then we retire for life. How about it, big shot?" He turned to Willis. "Are you in?"

Willis gave him a dollar and walked away, looking for

the machine foreman. There was a high metallic whine in the air and, behind it, the heavy thump of the presses. But in him, a silence, a stillness.

Sophie! How he missed her.

He was walking down the corridor on his break when he saw her. She was quite far away, standing in an open door in a shaft of light. He ran down the aisle, leaping over the skids. She was here! She had come looking for him. But when he got to the door, there was no one there. His imagination had played a trick on him, but all that day he kept expecting to see her. And thinking what he would say to her. How he would make up with her. Maybe he'd just open his arms.

At lunch, the guys were still talking about the lottery. Willis went through the paper. Not a word about him. Nobody came up to talk to him about the race. Nobody paid any attention to him. He'd been famous for two days.

He turned the page and read the personals.

> Jason, please come back. You misunderstood. I said things I shouldn't have said. Things I didn't mean. Give me another chance. Your lover, Honeybee.
>
> Young, strong and willing female desperately anxious to make up with particular beautiful male. You know who you are, My Little Popsicle.
>
> Sugartoes: Somebody is sorry, sorry, sorry. Can't sleep. Can't eat. Can't work. Life has lost its meaning without you. Pleading for another chance. Babeee, remember the good times.

He used to think that once you were famous, everything was right about your life. You didn't have to worry anymore. You didn't have to prove anything. You didn't have to try to be anything. You were famous. It was like a place you wanted to go to. You just wanted to get there; it didn't matter how. Being there was what mattered.

Well. Now he was there. Or had been there. He'd been famous for two days. And how did he feel? He felt like Willis Pierce, sitting on a box, eating his sandwich and feeling lonely, let down, sorry for himself. The college's offer should have made him feel good, but it didn't. He hadn't told anybody about it. He didn't have anyone to tell about it.

That night Willis drove over to Sophie's house. He parked in front and sat there, looking up at her windows. There were two windows facing the parking lot and they were both dark. It was magic he was hoping for, sitting there and waiting for the light to come on.

After a while, he went in and up the stairs. Her door was locked. There were circulars jammed under the door. He stood in the dark hallway and knocked. "Sophie?" Softly at first, then louder. "Sophie. It's me, Willis."

He leaned his head against the door and imagined the personals he would slip, one by one, under her door.

> Sophie, please come back. You misunderstood. I said things I shouldn't have said. Things I didn't mean. Give me another chance. Your Willy.
>
> Young, strong and willing male desperately anxious to make up with special beautiful female in his life. Sophie, remember the good times?
>
> Sweet Sophie Browne: Somebody is sorry, sorry, sorry. Can't sleep. Can't eat. Can't work. Life has lost its meaning without you. Pleading for another chance. Sophie, you are the girl of my dreams.

Willis drove home down East Broadway. Passing Spring Street he drove by the closed stand. The shutters were down; the newsstand was padlocked for the night. He drove on. Sophie wasn't here, she wasn't at her apartment, she wasn't anywhere in the city. And he didn't want to be in the city, either.

He drove up Broad, then swung up onto the overpass and out onto I-95, heading north. He was humming under his breath, one hand lightly on the wheel. It was dark and there were other cars on the road. He drove fast, concentrating on his driving, moving smoothly from one lane to another. He was just driving, enjoying himself.

Going for a ride, he said to himself.

It wasn't till he passed Four Corners and crossed the river bridge that he admitted to himself that he was on his way to see Sophie.

Forty-Three

Sophie's feet were burning inside her rubber boots. She carried the milk for the cats into the barn, but she didn't put on the lights. A storm was coming. As she filled the pan, the cats brushed up against her. She stood looking down the long central corridor of the barn to the square opening at the end. Wind, great scoops of air, spilled through the barn.

In the milk house, she hosed down the floor and wondered if Brenda was remembering to water her plants.

When she was done, she went outside and looked up the road. The sky was heavy and thick with clouds. Insects swarmed around the mercury light. There was a crack of lightning, and Jupiter started barking. Lightning and then thunder and then lightning again. In the flash, she saw a man standing in the road.

Willis's car had broken down at a crossroad in the middle of empty, uninviting country. Not a sign, not a house.

He and Zola had walked the rest of the way. As they came over the last rise, there was thunder and lightning, and he saw the farm, the sprawling, faded barns and the unfamiliar machinery. Then he saw Sophie.

He stopped. In the distance, she looked imposing, powerful and forbidding in her high black rubber boots.

A big fawn-colored dog was barking. Zola ran forward and the two dogs, the big dog and the little dog, circled each other and sniffed. A man came out of the house and went past Sophie into the barn.

Nothing was the way he'd imagined. Just getting to her, barely farther than crossing the road seemed impossible. Seemed harder than getting into the race. Than anything he'd ever done.

I don't have to do this, Willis thought. I can leave right now, just turn around and go back home, not do this thing.

She hadn't asked him to come. Did she want him? Did she want to hear anything he had to say? She hadn't believed him before. Why would she believe him now? What could he say that he hadn't said before? That he'd run the race? And a good race. What difference would that make to her? Everything about her said, keep your distance.

Zola saw Sophie and went crazy. She jumped up, her tail wagging and her mouth open, barking and laughing. Willis watched with envy. It was so easy for Zola. She was all feeling, all action. Her heart was like a spring that nothing could hold down.

Sophie was looking at him.

Then the rain started. Big, slow drops spattered in the road and fell on his head. He didn't move. It was as if everything he wanted, everything he needed to do, everything he wanted to say was locked inside him and there was no door and there was no key and there was no way out.

He'd come all this way and there was only the width of the road separating them, and he couldn't take another step. He looked at Sophie and then he looked back down the road the way he'd come and then he looked at Sophie again.

"Sophie," he said. "Sophie. I—I'm so glad . . ." He held his hands out. "It's raining," he said.

"Hello, Willis," she said.

"Hello, Sophie."

"Where's the car?"

"Broke down. It's a miracle I got as far as I did."

"Have you seen Brenda?"

"Once. She told me you were here."

"I'm glad you brought Zola."

He took a step toward her. "Are you glad I came?"

She nodded and moved toward him. It wasn't what she intended to do at all. She had meant to be cool, very cool. When she had thought about this moment—and she had thought about it constantly—she had told herself she wasn't going to let her feelings be pulled around, jerked this way and that way.

She'd been waiting for him, expecting him every day, sure he would come and just as sure she would never see him again. She kept rehearsing what she'd say. It was always the same thing. He'd hurt her and she didn't want to be hurt again.

Her brother came out of the barn and saw them. "It's raining," he said. He walked by them, and they went into the barn.

There was another crack of lightning and then a clap of thunder. A moment later the lights went out and it was black.

"Sophie?" Willis said. "Where are you?"

"I'm here."

"Damn!"

She could hear him stamping his feet. "What happened, Willis?"

"I stepped in it," he said. "Your cows! What do I do now?"

She found him and took his hand. "Come on." He followed her to the milk room. "Take off your sneakers." She dropped them into a pail of water. It was his bare feet that did her in. In the dark they seemed so pale and defenseless.

She took his hand and led him out of the wind to where the grain and the baled straw was stacked, and they sat down. "Are you cold?" She wrapped burlap around his feet.

"I was waiting for you to come back," he said.

"I was waiting for you to come here."

"I didn't think you'd listen to anything I said."

"I was mad at you for a long time," she said. "I'm still mad at you."

"Do you want me to go?"

"No . . . yes."

"Which one?"

"I don't know. That's why I left. I couldn't live that way, hating you and thinking about you all the time."

"I thought about you all the time, too." He wanted to take her hand. He wanted to touch her. He ached to put his arms around her. "I missed you every day," he said. "Every minute of every day."

He thought about the park where he'd heard the music,

and the race and after the race. He'd been looking for her, talking to her in his head, needing to talk to her. He wanted to say so much to her. He wanted to tell her it wasn't going to be the way it was before. He'd changed. He was different. He was still Willis Pierce, but he was different.

He'd done something that he'd never thought he could do. He'd proved something to himself. He could change. He'd run the race, he'd run against Aaron Hill. He'd done something he'd dreamed of and been afraid of. He'd done it to prove to her that he didn't have to be the way he was, that he could do something else, be somebody else.

That was what he'd come up here to tell her. He wanted to tell her about the race and the scholarship. Who else could he tell who would know what it meant to him? But most of all he wanted to tell her about the way he felt about her, and he didn't know if he could say it.

"I missed you," he said. "Sophie, please . . ." Rain battered the tin roof. It sounded like barrels rolling on the roof.

"What?" she yelled.

"I love you!"

He pointed to himself, to her, then put his hand over his heart. "You . . . me . . ."

She flung her arms around him and whispered in his ear.

Above them, the rain raced down the gutters like apples down a chute.

Later, when the lights came on, Sophie went back to her work. She shoveled grain into a wheelbarrow. Then she handed the shovel to Willis and wheeled the barrow toward the stanchions. He followed her, and while she grained the cows, he read her Bunny Fried's newspaper article about him.

She took the article from him and read it herself. "I didn't know that," she said. "You did it, Willis!"

"I thought you knew I ran."

"No, I didn't."

"I was sure I saw you. I ran for you. I ran the race and you were watching me."

"I wasn't there," she said. "I wish I had been." She smoothed the article. "Can I keep this?" She folded it and put it into her pocket.

Forty-Four

In the Spring Street Diner, Sophie is sitting by the window, waiting for Willis. It's raining outside and the window is fogged over. George is sweeping, closing up. Two white plastic bags of garbage are by the door.

Sophie sips her cocoa slowly. It's warm in the diner and she's tempted by the pie rack. The apple pie looks good, but so does the blueberry. "George," she says, "can you give me half a slice of apple pie?"

"And what do I do with the other half, darling?"

"I'll save it for my boyfriend."

George brings her the pie on two plates. She takes tiny bites, making the pie last. Ever since she and Willis came back to the city together, she has felt herself torn between pleasure and worry. Things are good between them. They are very good. They are wonderful. She's happy, but the little bit of worry is always there, the little bit of uncertainty.

Today is the end of her first week on her new job. She

is still surprised every time she thinks of what she is doing. When she came back from the farm, she didn't even know if Carl would give her her old job back. At best, she thought, he would put her back on the newsstand.

But the first day he drove her all over town in his blue Mercedes, showing her the apartment buildings he owned. He had a clipboard beside him, a yellow pad. He was following up a list of tenant complaints. One tenant was sick of waiting for his new shower head. Another complained that her neighbor was leaving the kids' bikes in the hall and creating a fire hazard. And someone else complained about not enough storage space.

"I don't have time for all this petty garbage, Sophie. I've got more important things to do. What about that shower head? I haven't got it. What am I supposed to do?"

"Why don't you let the tenant buy his own shower head and give you the bill?"

"What about those bikes in the hall? There're fire regulations. It'll be my neck."

"Can you make a bike room in the cellar? Divide up the space?"

"That's going to cost money."

"Not that much. You just need some two-by-fours, Sheetrock and a door with a lock. Anybody could do that. I could."

She didn't think her ideas were that great. They were just common sense, but over lunch, he offered her a job as his roving super and troubleshooter. More responsibility, more money and the use of a car.

She took the job.

Now in the diner, she's making a list of things she's got to do tomorrow.

When Willis comes in, he's full of excitement. He'll explain in a minute. "Got a pencil, Soph?" He kisses her. He sits down and eats the pie and then asks George for a sandwich and more pie. He borrows Sophie's notebook and starts figuring.

"I was up at the college today. That scholarship really is going to pay everything, but you know what I forgot to ask them? What about Zola? Am I going to be able to keep her in the dorm with me? Yeah, probably, I see dogs all over the place." Then he laughs. "Can you imagine me living in a dorm with college kids?"

"Zola can always come live with me," Sophie says and gets close and looks at his scribbles. "You going to tell me what that's all about?"

"You remember the emergency fund I was talking about? For my mother? In case something happens to her or to my father while I'm in school and she needs money? She's only got me to turn to."

Sophie nods. She knows about this.

"I asked Miholic for overtime for the rest of the summer, and I'm going to get a weekend job. An ice-cream truck. I'll probably sell the car. We can use yours, okay?"

"Lady and gentleman," George says, "the kitchen is closing in fifteen more minutes."

"Thank you," Sophie says.

Willis is still figuring. "I can save a little by cutting out movies, Soph. The stinger is my rent. If I could get a cheaper place until I start school. . . . What are you paying over there at Brenda's?"

"Almost the same as you. We should eat together more, that would save money. And I'll take you to the movies."

"Listen, I've got this great idea. I thought of it on the way over. It's going to solve the whole thing for me." He put a finger on her hand. "One, I give up my apartment. Two, I camp out with you."

"My place?"

"Don't you think it's a terrific idea? I don't take up a lot of room. You won't even know I'm there."

She laughs. "I always know when you're there."

"Two can live as cheap as one," he says.

"Saving money isn't a good reason to move in together," she says.

"That's not the only reason I want to live with you."

"We haven't even talked about it."

"It would only be temporary," he says.

"You know that's kind of insulting. I'm not a motel."

"You mean you want me to move in for good?"

"I didn't say that."

"You don't want me to move in at all?"

"You make it sound like I'm denying you something. What if we don't get along?"

"We're going to get along. We always get along."

"Oh, sure. Short memory, Willis. This is a serious thing. Maybe it's too soon for us. Besides . . ." She hesitates, thinking that she's been on her own for only a little while. She's still figuring things out for herself, and having Willis around won't make it easier.

She knows herself: She'd start depending on him to make up her mind for her. She definitely doesn't feel positive enough about living together to say yes. Not just like that. Not now. Not this soon. Sure, it sounds nice, but—and there are a lot of buts and what-ifs.

What if they get in each other's way? What if he wants to eat pizza three times a day? What if she wants to stay up when he goes to sleep? Her place is tiny. Weekends, she likes to sleep in and he gets up at the crack of dawn. And it doesn't mean just the two of them in that little apartment, it means Zola, too.

Sophie doesn't want to be selfish, but she doesn't want them to make a mistake, either. "Living together, we could end up hating each other." He doesn't say anything, and she can see he's disappointed. She jiggles his arm. "Say something."

"What am I supposed to say? You don't want to live with me."

"That's what I was afraid you'd say. You've got it all wrong. Do you think I'm being selfish?"

"Yes," he says.

"Because I'm not giving you what you want, that makes me selfish?"

"You asked."

"But you—you're not being selfish?" she says, and it feels and it smells and it sounds like they're off to a fight.

"That's right," he says. "What's the big deal about living together for a few months?"

"Lady and gentleman, I'm closed now," George says.

Willis zips up his jacket. "What do you say?"

"I wish we weren't fighting."

"You don't want us to live together? You don't want me to move in?"

She shakes her head.

He pulls his collar up like a turtleneck and puts his hands in his pockets.

Sophie puts on her jacket, and they go out.

Outside, they're not talking, but they're not going away from each other, either. They start walking. It's raining and they're not talking and Willis is feeling bad, because it feels like all the other times they fought. All day he couldn't wait to see Sophie and tell her this great idea and then it turns out to be a rotten idea.

They walk over to Broadway together. Finally, he says, "If it was my place, I'd probably feel the same way."

"Maybe you wouldn't," she says, and links her arm with his.

"I would if it was a bum idea." He puts his arm around her. "Guess what, Sophie. I was doing something unusual. I was just thinking about me."

"Oh, you're not that bad," she says, and gives him a loving look.

Being close with someone isn't easy, he thinks. It's not just a matter of saying I love you. When you're with somebody else, when you like that person and love that person, you have to think about them as much as you think about yourself. If easy is what you want, he says to himself, then be alone and all you'll have to think about is you.

And he remembers how it was before Sophie, alone in that box of a room, alone with his radio and his dreams of running and dreams of a girl he created out of thin air, a girl who never was.

And he leans in toward Sophie and brings her closer to him. "Which way?" he says.

They stand there undecided for a moment, then with their arms around each other, they run toward Sophie's place.